# THE HUSBAND EXPERIENCE

## SWEET SOUTHERN
## BOOK 1

### MAYA JEAN

Copyright © 2024 by Maya Jean

All rights reserved.

No part of this book may be reproduced in any form or by any electronic or mechanical means, including information storage and retrieval systems, without written permission from the author, except for the use of brief quotations in a book review.

The story, all names, characters, and incidents portrayed in this production are fictitious. No identification with actual persons (living or deceased), places, buildings, and products is intended or should be inferred.

Beta read by Sage, Lexi, Devin, and Donatella

Edited by L.C. Valentine

Proofread by Judy's Proofreading

Cover by Black Jazz Design

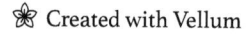

❦ Created with Vellum

*For Aiden,*
*You were my first, but you won't be my last.*

# CONTENT AND TRIGGER WARNINGS

- Mild dom/sub undertones
- Primal play
- Death of a spouse from cancer
- Death of an extended relative
- Sex work

# PLAYLIST

- You Stay by the Sea by Axel Flovent
- Dancing After Death by Matt Maeson
- Midnight by Paper Planes
- Keep Me by Novo Amor
- This Could be by Joel Ansett
- To Begin Again by Ingrid Michelson and Zayn
- This is how you fall in love by Jeremy Zucker and Chelsea Cutler
- Carry Me Home by sod ven
- No One Could Ever Love Me Like You by Imaginary Future
- To Build a Home by The Cinematic Orchestra
- I Found by Amber Run
- I Can't Make You Love Me by Teddy Swims
- For Me, It's You by Lo Moon
- Obvious by CHPTRS
- Part of Me by By The Coast
- Same Boat by Lizzy McAlpine
- Touch by Sleeping At Last

*Playlist*

- I Don't Want to Let You Go by Jordan Hart
- Vienna - Acoustic by Bailey Rushlow
- One Moment More by Mindy Smith
- Three by Sleeping at Last
- Say It First by Sam Smith
- Make You Feel My Love by Sleeping At Last
- Simply The Best by Billianne
- Let the New Begin by CHPTRS

# PROLOGUE
## COLBY

Loss has become a part of me. Sometimes loss is a spark on fragile kindling that triggers a blazing wildfire. But like new growth sprouts through burnt earth afterwards, new life comes eventually.

Trust me, I've become kind of an expert on grief in the past few years. I lost my husband and my uncle in a short span of time. My family is tight-knit, so the loss of both men reverberated through us, shaking our usually firm foundation.

My footsteps echo loudly as I walk through the house towards the hallway that contains all my family pictures. The house I designed and built just for myself, without anyone else in mind.

I come to a slow stop at the picture of Marcus and me on our wedding day. That day had been perfect, perfectly frozen in my memory. My smile in the picture is bright as always, but Marcus' is softer, a private one meant just for me. His smile used to feel so earned to me, like by making Marcus grin, I'd accomplished some great feat.

The pain of losing him has turned into a dull ache, less glass-edge sharp than only a year ago. This subsiding pain is just another sign to me that I'm ready to move forward. My still tender heart leaves me in a sort of limbo—one foot in, one foot out—ready to try again.

Just earlier in the day I took off my wedding ring for the final time, tucking it away in a drawer of my dresser. The action was the last of many steps of letting myself move forward. I won't say "move on," but moving forward feels better, more accurate. To maybe try again. But going on dates … doing the entire thing … I don't know if I'm ready for that.

I wish the universe could just give me the perfect someone without having to search for them. Life is never that easy though.

My Irish setter, Whiskey, barks and startles me out of my reverie when my front door gingerly pushes open.

"Colby?" my cousin Beau calls out from the front entrance.

I pad barefoot down the hallway with my hands shoved deep into my jeans pockets. My cousin is standing by the front door, patiently waiting for me to come into view. Beau's been a steady rock for me the past few years, visiting almost every Sunday on his way home from the family farm.

"Hey." My voice comes out scratchy, even to my own ears. Hot shame wells up inside me for just a moment before disappearing, this is Beau, it's alright for him to witness my grief.

"Colby," Beau says softly, voice full of tender empathy. He takes his ball cap off, rubbing at the dark brown hairs standing up on the top of his head. "Bad day?"

A helpless shrug is all I can give Beau in answer. Bad days are far and few between now, but they still come. Less out of sadness these days and more out of loneliness. Some days the distinct lack of noise in my house is so overwhelming that I could weep.

Beau quietly follows me into the kitchen. After handing Whiskey a small treat, I fondly pat her head. I grab a beer out of the fridge to hand to Beau. Silence surrounds us for a bit as we stand sharing beers and company.

Whiskey is a solid presence by my feet just like she has been the past few years. She'd been a present from Marcus before I'd lost him. *To keep you company*, Marcus had said with a wry smile. The unsaid *once I'm gone*, had almost killed me then, but I'm grateful for his sweet thoughtfulness now.

"How's your mom?" I ask Beau as I take a slow sip of my beer.

It's easier to focus on my aunt, on Beau, because their grief is fresher, much sharper than mine. Beau's always been a quiet kind of guy, tenderhearted too. I'm a few years older than him, so I've always been a protector of sorts for him, despite him towering over me even by the time we were teens.

"Mom's doing good. She's working back in the front office again." Beau takes a steadying sip of his own beer. "Listen, I got a suggestion for you. But you gotta not be judgmental."

I skewer him with the most intense look I can summon. "Beau, it's me. I was there that time you jumped naked into the springs on a dare when you were a kid."

"True," Beau says with a hearty chuckle.

I hold my beer out, using it to gesture for Beau to go on.

"Maybe you need to get back in the saddle. Get back out there. Just pull the Band-Aid off."

"That's a lot of metaphors, Beau."

"Shut up." Beau shoots me a crooked smile as he belly

laughs. I've missed his laugh so much the last few months. "Do you remember Trevor?"

"Yeah," I tell him, rubbing at my unshaven jaw as I recall Beau's last boyfriend. "That guy you brought to Andy's wedding? To your dad's funeral too. What happened to him?"

Beau lets out a deep breath, then tiredly rests his forearms on the kitchen island. Exhaustion radiates off of him, and I wish I could help him, but I don't know how. He anxiously taps his fingers against the beer bottle he cradles in his hands. Clearly he wants to share with me but is unsure. So I wait him out.

"Listen, I hired him."

"You hired him," I repeat in confusion.

"He was a fake boyfriend. I hired him for the wedding and again for the funeral."

I laugh and shake my head in utter disbelief. This is nothing like Beau. "Why the hell would you do that?"

Beau stands up again, anxiously running his hand over his head. He paces a little in the kitchen, then turns his heartsick gaze back to me. "Dad was so sick, and Mom was worried shitless, and I wanted them to think I was happy. I wanted Dad to die thinking I was happy."

"Oh, Beau."

My heart simultaneously aches for him and me. Both of us are so torn apart by grief for very different reasons. Beau sends me a sad, miserable sort of smile before grabbing his beer to finish it off in just a few gulps. He places the empty beer on the island, aiming a narrow-eyed, serious look at me.

"I think you should do it."

"Do what?"

"Hire a fake boyfriend. You got that week off in early July

because you close the firm." I go to stop him, but Beau holds out a hand for me to keep listening. "Take that week off and play boyfriend, feel alive again. Maybe it'll help you get out of your funk, move on a little bit. Not that I'm telling you to move on from Marcus after a week playing boyfriend, but you know what I mean. We all loved him, but we love you too."

I think those are the most words I've ever heard Beau say at once. I nod at him, taking his argument into serious consideration. He claps my shoulder in his large hand, squeezes firmly once, then leaves without another word. Which is just so Beau.

I watch him slowly disappear up my driveway. Beau easily jumps over the fence, finally vanishing out of my sight towards his own property.

Whiskey looks up at me begging for another treat, so I give her one because she's the best girl. My mind whirs with thoughts about what Beau just told me. A fake boyfriend? Trevor had seemed so in love with Beau, it had seemed so real. My phone vibrates in my pocket. I pull my phone out to find a text from Beau with the contact information for the agency.

*The Boyfriend Experience.*

I finish my Sunday night chores around the house with an anxious heart. Cook dinner for myself, get ready for the week ahead. All the usual things that keep me busy and my mind elsewhere.

Once I'm in bed for the night with Whiskey curled up at my feet, I stare at my phone like it could catch on fire.

Do I dare do it? Do I hire a fake boyfriend for a week? I pull up a photo of me and Marcus from our last vacation. Our last bit of joy before everything went to shit. I can basically hear Marcus in my head telling me to do it. Hear him teasing me for even waiting so long. That familiar teasing voice is all the confirmation I need.

The business is sleek, I'll give them that. The owner, a young curly-haired blonde, talks about how she started the business with her best friend during college. He was the fake boyfriend and she ran behind the scenes. It goes on and on for a bit about the level of professional boyfriend they aim to provide from wedding dates, to work outings, to just for the weekend. My heart beats wildly in my chest as I realize I'm really going to do this. I'm going to hire a fake boyfriend.

The website has a survey to fill out. It's very thorough, not just for what I expect in a boyfriend, but what the boyfriend can expect from me. The survey even goes as far as to ask about kinks and preferences. Maybe I can also explore some of the kinks I haven't explored in years, ones that Marcus didn't love, so I easily abandoned them. We experimented a lot, but there were things I left behind when we got together. It was never a hardship, because I loved Marcus. But it could be exhilarating to try them again after so many years.

The whole process doesn't take as long as I expected. However, typing out just a few sentences zaps all the energy from me. I turn onto my side to stare at the wall of my bedroom. Sleep comes for me, but it takes a while. Thoughts of my future fake boyfriend filter into my dreams that night. The promise of something unexpected on my horizon. Maybe something great.

# 1

## ELI

An annoying buzz wakes me up from a deep, peaceful sleep. I appear to have fallen asleep at my desk. Again. For the millionth time. A groan escapes me as I roughly rub at my stupidly numb cheek. How am I twenty-eight but still fall asleep within moments of sitting down at my desk? The soft blue light of a computer screen might as well be a damn night-light for me.

The annoying buzzing gets angrier. I blink the lingering, hazy sleep from my eyes. Somehow my phone is always at the scene of the crime. My phone screen flashes in the darkness of my office and I let out a loud sigh at the sight of Trevor's name. He's a fellow boyfriend and also one of my best friends, so this call could go either way. Is it work related or is he coming out of a late evening showing of a movie and needs me to chaperone him on his walk home?

"Trevor."

"Eli," Trevor whispers, an edge of urgency in his sweet voice. "I need a huge favor."

Trevor sounds breathless, voice a little shakier than I'm

used to hearing it. He might be the youngest of us all, but he's notoriously made of steel. Nothing shakes Trevor. Never a client and not much else.

"What's up?"

Trevor lets out a loud, tired breath. "I need you to take a job for me."

My frown deepens because this *never* happens. We take the jobs we're assigned because the agency carefully pairs us up with boyfriends. If Trevor is handing someone off to me, then he either knows them in a good way … or a bad way. I want to pry, but knowing Trevor, I won't like the answer I get anyway.

"I just forwarded you an email the service got earlier today. Claire initially thought of me, but she's wrong. There is literally no one else on the team besides you that could take this job."

Claire is the hard-ass owner of The Boyfriend Experience, the agency that I—in very loose terms—freelance for once in a while. The job pays enough that I can focus on completing my PhD program eighty percent of the time and there's no other job like that on earth. Plus, it helps that I'm pretty good at being a boyfriend. A fake one at least. I like sex too, so it's a win-win for me most of the time.

I open the email on my phone and lean back in my desk chair to read it with Trevor on speaker.

Name: Colby Smith

Age: 39 years old

Kinks: I prefer to be dominant in all scenarios. Also, spanking and primal play if the boyfriend is amenable to it.

Sex included in boyfriend experience: Yes

Length of time: First week of July
Lodging: Wherever the boyfriend wants
Comments: See below

Dear The Boyfriend Experience,

*I am hoping you can help me. My cousin Beau recommended you to me after he used your services last year. He had nothing but nice things to say, which is a rarity for my cousin. I am writing in for a very particular request. I was wondering if you offer the husband experience? I am looking for someone to let me love them, and love me back, and I want all the romance in the world. All expenses for the husband will of course be paid as I'd like this to be a real vacation. We can go anywhere in the world the husband wants as long as he's willing to love me the entire week. Money is no issue.*

Thanks,
   *Colby*

The pain in the email is so evident, so raw. To ask to be loved by a stranger for an entire week is an extraordinary act of courage.

Maybe I am the guy for the job, because nothing sounds better to me. An entire week-long paid vacation just to play husband, to give someone love and care? Sounds perfect. If the dates don't interfere with my schedule, then it's definitely something I can do. Something I want to do.

"Were any other details provided?" I ask softly.

Trevor hums thoughtfully into the phone. "The first week of July."

I pull up my schedule on my phone. Summer is great for me because I don't usually teach a class. Instead, I focus on my research.

"The first week of July works. Pay?"

"Money is no issue said the man ..." Trevor trails off with a low, bitter chuckle. "Name your price, hubby."

That does get my attention, but there's another key factor at play. "Limits?"

"Just the standards," Trevor says, a little more awkwardly than he normally would. "This guy really does sound right up your alley. You're the best of all of us."

I restlessly tap my fingers against the desk in deep contemplation. A week of nonstop acting like a husband, twenty-four seven. I'm not even sure I know how to quantify that really. The most I've ever been paid was ten thousand dollars for playing boyfriend to a closeted rockstar for an evening of debauchery.

"Thirty thousand dollars for the week?" I ask, hoping for confirmation from Trevor.

"Great!" Trevor says with a clear smile in his voice. That's the Trevor I know. "I will let Claire know she'll need to tell Colby that you'll cost him fifty thousand dollars for the entire week."

"Wait—"

"Bye!" Trevor yells before I can argue with him.

I pull my phone away from my face and frown anxiously down at it. Fifty thousand dollars feels a little like highway robbery to me. Trevor is probably already telling Claire to email the poor guy back with the price. Colby will surely reply that the company is out of our mind.

## The Husband Experience

Feeling helpless, I go about my evening. A bowl of cereal for dinner. A shower hot enough to melt off my skin. A perfect evening. Until I have to deal with my hair. My curls never want to cooperate with me. I spend a few minutes trying to tame my pesky curls, before giving up and going about my nightly skincare routine.

Just as I'm finishing brushing my teeth, my phone lights up on the bathroom counter. I lean against the counter to anxiously peer down at my screen. The message preview reads *APPROVED - THE HUSBAND EXPERIENCE* and I feel a little tingle of nerves in the pit of my belly. Fifty thousand dollars for one week of playing husband wherever I choose. Doesn't seem that hard to me.

I think for a moment about all the places we could go. I could choose anything. A week on the Italian coast, an island in Greece, the rainforest in South America ... but what if my future husband doesn't like any of those places? If I'm going to play doting husband for the week, I figure maybe I should start a little early.

My toothbrush dangles out of the corner of my mouth as I type out a quick email. I set my phone down with a delighted smirk. This guy will be melting in my hands before we even meet up. Every cent of that fifty thousand dollars will be earned.

---

I ALMOST FORGET about the upcoming husband experience since the only reminder I have is the notation in my calendar. The reminder comes in abruptly at the end of June when Claire forwards me an email with the location of choice. Colby's chosen a gorgeous beach house for the week.

But Florida? My eyes basically roll back into my brain. Of all the places in the world, I'm going to have to spend a week playing husband in the armpit of America. Great. Superb. Excellent.

The address is for a very expensive beach home, per my googling. It's not a rental, which surprises me. Further googling shows that the house was bought years ago for a cool couple million dollars. Not too shabby.

On the bright side, I don't have to catch a long flight to get where I'm going, considering I live in Georgia. I'll just make the five-hour drive down, listen to some beachy country songs, and then I'll also have my car in case I need to make a fast escape.

I pack a wide array of outfits from beachy to dressy to slutty in hopes that I pack something that makes my fake husband happy. I'm well used to dressing for my boyfriends.

The drive passes by quickly as I blare a random playlist of beach music through my car's Bluetooth. I roll the windows down as I approach the water, unable to hold myself back from feeling the glorious ocean breeze on my face.

My GPS directs me to come to a stop in front of a three-story light blue beach house. Everything about the place screams beach, from the color of the house, to the white rocking chairs on the balconies, and the wide-open windows that show me a view of the breathtaking ocean beyond. For just a moment, I stand there taking in the scent, letting the salty air wash over me like a balm.

After grabbing my suitcase out of the car, I take the weathered stairs up to the entrance of the house. I consider knocking for a brief moment, but that doesn't seem like something a husband would do. Wouldn't a husband just walk right into his own vacation home? So I take a deep, steadying breath and push through the heavy front door.

The house is eerily quiet. If I hadn't seen the car out front, I would assume that the house is empty.

I drop my suitcase by the front entrance and start to explore the large house. Everything inside is white but there are light and dark blue accents throughout. The house radiates calm. The inside smells just like the outside, like the ocean and warm salt air. The sound of the waves breaking against the shore echoes through the house. I run my fingers through my unruly hair, hoping it's still as presentable as it was when I styled it earlier in the morning.

Movement from the balcony at the back of the house gets my attention. A man slowly stands from where he'd been leaning against the railing. All I can see is broad shoulders, a strong back, and sandy-blond hair. Even without seeing his face, he's not what I thought he was going to be.

As if Colby senses my gaze on him, he slowly turns around. Our eyes lock through the large window facing the ocean. An odd shiver rolls its way through my body. I swallow loudly and my fingers twitch aimlessly at my side.

Colby is breathtakingly gorgeous. Bigger than me by a few inches and also quite a bit broader. One or two days' worth of stubble dots his square jaw. I've been paid by a lot of people to have sex with them and usually I get by with faking attraction, just worrying about making the experience good for them.

I won't have to do any faking with Colby.

He aims one last look at the ocean over his shoulder, then opens the sliding glass door to come inside.

"Elijah?" Colby asks with a crooked smile.

Oh no. He's got a deep voice and a southern accent. My two greatest weaknesses. He might as well be my kryptonite.

"Yes."

Colby smiles softly. His entire face warms with his grin, even the crow's feet at the corners of his eyes are endearing. He radiates kindness, something I rarely get in these experiences.

Colby clears his throat awkwardly. "Hello, husband."

I swallow again, feeling all sorts of unmoored. "Eli."

"Eli?" Colby asks with a little furrow between his eyebrows. God, even that is cute. Holy hell.

"Yes," I say after clearing my throat. "My husband should call me Eli."

A wicked smile crosses Colby's face as he steps just a little closer. Oh God. He smells amazing too, like expensive, musky cologne and something earthy. Like the smell in the air before a storm. A large hand comes up to caress my face, his thumb tilts my head up so that our gazes meet.

"Alright, husband." His dark blue eyes shift between mine, looking straight into me. "It's nice to meet you, Eli. Are you ready to be mine for a week?"

I nod because suddenly my mouth is too dry for me to even attempt forming words. My mouth is basically the Sahara. Colby just smiles as if he knows exactly how hard my brain is short-circuiting at the very sight of him. He dips down to press a gentle kiss to the hinge of my jaw, then slowly pulls away. Tangling our fingers together, he tugs me towards the kitchen.

"Want something to drink?" Colby asks, grabbing a cold bottle of water from the fridge. The man doesn't even wait for me to answer. Instead, he just hands me the bottle after opening it for me.

*The Husband Experience*

The cold water does a good job waking my brain back up after I quickly gulp half of it down. I don't usually get so tongue-tied around people. Talking isn't an issue for me, I never feel off-center, and I always know what to say ... but looking at Colby has me all sorts of messed up. I don't know how else to explain it. His presence is a lightning strike to my nervous system.

Colby takes my hand back in his and starts to show me the house. He's got great arms. Great everything really. His hair is the perfect shade of ashy blond, the kind I always wished for as a young kid, because I got stuck with my biological father's dark hair, skin tone, and everything else.

I also notice he's barefoot. Something about that sets me more at ease, even though I can't explain why. Colby's muscles move under his shirt as he tugs me along behind him. I want to *climb* him.

"This is our bedroom," Colby tells me with a gesture of his arm. I try very hard to not get caught up in the sight of his tanned, thick forearms. They're work hardened, and I like that. More than I should.

The bedroom faces the back of the house, towards the ocean. There's floor-to-ceiling windows so that the view of the water is unimpeded. A king-size bed faces the gulf, sitting against the opposite wall. I bet getting fucked here is going to be amazing.

I send a smirk Colby's way. "So many memories in this room."

Colby's face shutters for a moment before that pleasant smile returns. "Yes and more to come. Now the bathroom is to the left. There's a staircase from the balcony that'll take you right down to the beach. It's a private beach, so it's only ours."

"I've never been fucked by the beach before," I murmur softly, mostly to myself.

"We'll remedy that," Colby says quickly, without a trace of humor.

A shiver rolls down my spine again. Colby disappears back downstairs while I check out the bathroom. Much like the rest of the house, it's all white tiles and blue accents with a large walk-in shower built to accommodate four people at a time. I can't wait to try it out. A large clawfoot bathtub sits in front of the window facing the waves. Everything about this place screams romance and relaxation.

Colby returns a moment later with my suitcase in tow.

"Want to see the ocean?"

"Sure …" I trail off as I look at him. "Should I be ready? I'm not sure if you've done this before but it's no different than fucking a boyfriend. You'll have to let me know so I can prepare."

A look of confusion washes over Colby's face. "I'll prep you. Do you normally prep yourself?"

I let out a contrite laugh. "If I don't prepare myself, then half the time it wouldn't be remotely enjoyable for me. It's fine, I can do it."

"No," Colby says firmly with a frown. His chest even puffs out a little bit. "I'll prepare you while you're with me. You can do everything leading up to it in the privacy of the bathroom if that's also what you're asking."

"Alright," I agree, not quite sure what else to say.

Colby nods once, pleased. "Now let's go look at the ocean. I'll cook dinner later and we can eat it on the porch as we get to know one another better."

I follow Colby down the stairs from the balcony of the bedroom. The warm summer breeze blows across my face, making me smile. Both sides of the beach are empty with dunes rising and falling, giving the appearance of us being alone. I take my shoes off at the bottom of the stairs, leaving them there before walking out towards the waves. Another smile crosses my face when the warm water brushes against my toes.

Colby comes up beside me, his presence heavy and warm. In the most lovely sort of way. He shoots me another gentle smile that awakens millions of butterflies in my belly. Tucking his hands in the pockets of his jeans, he stares thoughtfully out at the horizon.

I'm meant to play husband with this man for a week but he's still a total enigma. Usually, I get a brief about the person I'll be playing boyfriend to but I received nothing about Colby Smith. All I know is that he's paying a hefty amount for one no-holds-barred week with me and that he has an affinity for primal play, per his application.

I shiver again at the very idea.

"Cold?" Colby asks, voice concerned.

"No," I reply, making sure my voice is as husky as possible.

"Ah," Colby says with a knowing smile. "You like your job?"

I look away from him and back at the ocean. The man probably thinks all I am is a sex worker, that it's my full-time job. I'll let him think that. I never want the men I serve to know much about the real me because I don't want to shatter their illusion.

Most men want to have me for a brief time, they like the feeling that they're using me, that I'm something they can buy just for their pleasure. Shattering that illusion will only make the money they spend on me not feel put to good use. I know my value to them all, even Colby despite his shy smiles.

"Love it. It affords me a lot of freedom and I get to travel. I get to spend a week by the ocean with a lovely man who's going to fuck me silly."

Colby grunts, eyes scanning my body, and rocks back on his heels in a cute, shy sort of way. "They told me you're the sweetest boyfriend on the roster."

I snort inelegantly. "What that means is that I never get a bad review because I know how to make a customer happy."

"I'm your husband this week, not a customer," Colby says firmly, jaw tight. "I want to make you happy this week too."

I roll my eyes internally. "Of course, honey."

"No pet names."

"Got it," I say succinctly.

Colby pulls his hands out of his pockets and shakes his arms, like someone preparing to dive off a cliff. "I'm going to kiss you."

Oh wow, he's got to psych himself up for it. Great. I aim a reassuring smile at him as he turns towards me. I let him manhandle me into the circle of his arms. His chest is firm and broad against my own, sending a rush of warmth through me. There's just something about a man who's bigger and stronger than me that I love.

A hand tangles in the hair at the nape of my neck before he dips down to kiss me. I close my eyes against the onslaught of his lips on top of my own. He tastes like coffee and something that's probably just Colby. The kiss is lovely, one of the nicer ones I've experienced. But Colby is holding back. I can feel it in the tension of his shoulders, the absence of passion in his kiss.

Maybe he's nervous. I'm not sure.

I slide my hands up his arms to settle around his neck. Licking into his mouth, I tilt my head to deepen the kiss. The tension eases out of Colby's shoulders until he's kissing me with no restraint, like we've kissed a hundred times before. Now that's why I'm the favorite boyfriend. I love getting people to let go and relax enough to forget that they're paying for me.

Colby's fingers tighten painfully in my hair. He bites at my bottom lip, forcing me to let out an absolutely indecent moan. My brain shuts off for one glorious moment, then reboots quickly back online when Colby abruptly pulls away. I ache to chase after him, to kiss him again.

"That's a husband kiss for sure," Colby says, out of breath, eyes glazed over.

"Of course it is, we're husbands." I do my best to keep my voice even so he can't tell just how out of control his kiss made me. Calm. I'm totally calm.

He smiles softly at me. A little, unsure sort of smile but it's beautiful all the same. I rub my fingers through his stubble and tenderly brush my thumb under his eye. His eyes slowly close and his face tilts into my hand like it's the first time he's felt touch in years. Maybe it has been. Something about Colby tells me he's touch starved. Those are my favorite types of clients.

We walk hand in hand back up to the house. He grips my hand tight, and I let him. Once inside the house, we go our separate ways. Unpacking my suitcase is my first line of business. My shirts line up beside his in the closet. There's more of his clothes in there than I imagined for a week, but it's his home, so maybe he leaves clothes here. I'm careful to respect his space in the bedroom, only putting my essentials out in the bathroom.

My presence is clear but it's not overwhelming.

A little while later I find him in the kitchen preparing for dinner. His dark blue eyes flit up to me for a moment, before his gaze returns back to what he's doing at the kitchen island. An array of vegetables dot the countertop along with chicken breast marinating in a glass pan. Some sort of spiced rice bubbles on the gas stovetop behind Colby.

"Wow," I say in awe.

He winks good-naturedly at me. "Thank you. I love to cook."

I take a seat at the kitchen island. "Obviously, and it smells amazing. I can't wait to try it."

He slides some raw vegetables in a bowl across the counter to me. "If you're hungry."

I wink back at him and take a few pieces of chopped pepper to nibble on as he finishes preparing our dinner for the grill. Turning my gaze towards the ocean, I notice that the sun is dipping down to kiss the horizon. Nothing tops a sunset at the beach. The sky is turning a deep orange and the color invades the kitchen, warming the house even more.

Colby quietly heads out to the balcony to grill our dinner. I can't help but follow him, some unknown thing telling me to stay close. I lean against the railing as he gets started at the grill.

"God, that view is gorgeous," I whisper, mostly to myself.

"It is."

I glance over my shoulder at Colby to find him looking at me, not the sunset, and I flush under his weighty gaze. The sweet talking is appreciated although wholly unnecessary. I decide to not remind him I'm a sure thing. The smell of the dinner mixes with the smell of the ocean breeze creating an even more relaxing atmosphere. All my troubles just melt away.

"Dinner's ready," Colby calls out.

I turn from the railing and make my way over to take a seat at the table. A platter of grilled chicken, grilled vegetables, and some kind of dirty rice sits at the center of the table. My mouth instantly waters. I'm not much of a cook myself and neither was my mother. I've spent the last ten years living off of takeout, delivery, and pre-made meals from the organic grocery store down the street from my apartment.

I take one bite of the chicken and moan out loud.

Colby chuckles as he cuts his chicken. "Good?"

"So good," I say around a mouthful of food. I don't even care that I look ridiculous. I eat the food like it's my last meal on earth. It's that good. The right amount of spice and sweetness and the chicken is so tender that I almost cry. "Are you a cook?"

Colby shakes his head with a smile. "No, I just enjoy cooking. I'm an architect."

I eye him across the table. "That's always seemed like such a cool job to me."

"It is most of the time. A lot of responsibility too, though. If I design something badly, then people can be hurt. I have to carry a lot of liability insurance."

"You work for a design firm?"

Colby smirks at me over the table. "I own my own firm."

"Nice. You sound well off. Good for you."

"This week we're well off, remember."

I suppress the urge to roll my eyes and just smile sweetly at him. "Of course, husband."

Colby cocks his head at me as he slowly chews on a piece of chicken. "I'm paying for your company and your time but I don't want you to be fake with me for seven days. I'm sure you're used to putting on a show, putting on an act, but that's not what I'm paying for."

I lean back in my chair, now done with my dinner. "You could've gotten someone from a hookup app to play pretend with you for a week on a vacation. People buy me when they want something in particular. I'm giving you what you paid for."

"Yeah?" Colby asks, voice low, a little mean. "What did I pay for, Eli?"

"You paid for a husband who'll do whatever you want and one who'll keep you happy for six days of fucking by the beach. And that's what I'm going to give you. Take it or leave it."

Colby skewers me with a look so intense that I can't help but squirm a little in my seat. He continues to eat as I stew a little. Patience radiates off of him as if he's waiting me out, thinking I'll give in and admit something. I have no idea what that something is though.

I sit with my arms crossed over my chest, watching anxiously as he finishes his dinner. He stands with his plate in hand, grabs my plate, then goes inside to clean up. Figuring he left me alone to sulk, I stare up at the now pink and purple sky.

Fuck. What's wrong with me? I never talk to clients like that. I never do anything that might get me sent packing. Jesus, he's probably going to email Claire and ask for a different husband for the week. Well, I know it won't be Trevor because something about Colby sent him running. I also don't see Trevor consenting to being chased through the dunes and fucked into the sand like I will. I let out a ragged breath, then jump when I realize Colby is back outside with me.

He sets down a chilled glass of wine on the table in front of me. "Drink this and relax. I'm not fucking you tonight."

"Why not?" I ask petulantly.

"Because you're on edge for some reason and I want you to want it the first time I fuck you."

"I want it now. You're literally paying me to want this, Colby."

"Stop," Colby demands, voice low and firm. My mouth instantly slams shut. "I'm not playin' head games with you, Eli. Yes, I've paid for your company. Yes, I've paid to fuck you. But I don't want an act because then I won't enjoy it. I want you to be yourself. We will settle in together and then I'll fuck you tomorrow. I'll take you out to dinner tomorrow too like a good husband would after he fucks his husband's brains out. Got it?"

I'm struck speechless, so I just nod. A tendril of shame forms in the pit of my stomach, but I wash it away with a large gulp of the moscato Colby kindly gave me. I watch through the windows as he cleans up after dinner. The wine does relax me, and for some reason I cannot explain, it pisses me off that he knew that's what I needed. Because this man should not know me. This man does *not* know me.

After the kitchen is clean and the sun has fully set, the long drive earlier in the morning starts to wear on me. I'm so tired. Colby drags me to the bedroom, shocking me, because I'd assumed maybe I'd be sleeping in another bedroom.

He stands me at the end of the bed and proceeds to undress me. I open my mouth to argue with him but one look from him has me snapping my mouth back shut. Tenderly, without any heat, he undresses me and puts one of his larger

T-shirts over my head for me to sleep in. I'm so momentarily thrown by it all that I sway on my feet a little. Colby notices and ushers me into the bed, pulling the blankets up over me.

I lie there frozen, watching enraptured as he goes about his own night routine. He returns from the bathroom in only a pair of tight boxer briefs. My heart practically skyrockets through my chest at just the sight of him. He's so fucking hot. He's big and broad and there's a perfect amount of dark blond hair scattered across his chest, down his thighs, and on his legs. He's in incredible shape for a man his age.

Colby climbs into the bed beside me, turns onto his side, and proceeds to manhandle me into his arms. I like it though. Oddly. The soft sound of the waves echoes through the bedroom as Colby molds his body around mine. He's warm and firm against the line of my back. Against my better judgment, I fall asleep held in the circle of his arms.

# 2

## ELI

My first thought when I wake up is that my mouth is insanely dry. Soft sunlight filters through the windows when I blink my eyes open. The bed is cold, alerting me to the fact I'm alone. I'm eternally grateful for the solitude. I need to get my bearings. I need to start acting right too. More like the good boyfriend I usually am.

The door to the bedroom opens with a soft squeak to reveal Colby with a tray full of breakfast foods in his hands. I blink slowly at him as he approaches. He's shirtless and barefoot but wearing tattered sweatpants. Colby sets the tray down on the fluffy down blanket, right in front of me. He settles beside me on the bed with a shy smile, averting his gaze from mine.

"I made you breakfast. I didn't know what you like best, so I made a few different types of eggs. And there's pastries." Colby clears his throat awkwardly. "Tell me what you like and I'll make it for you the rest of the time you're here."

I angle my head towards him. We stare at each other for a few moments before I lean up to sweetly kiss his cheek. He smells like aftershave, but it's soft, like maybe he only used a little. I like it.

"Thank you," I say softly against his stubbled cheek. "I like my eggs over hard with a bagel."

"Alright," Colby murmurs against my own cheek. His hand sneaks up to brush the messy curls from my face as he pulls away. "There you are."

I smile at him—a real smile, not a forced one—and turn back to look at the tray. I grab a pastry and bite into it. We eat breakfast together quietly as the sun creeps further up the horizon. Sleeping isn't necessarily a difficult thing for me, but I can't say the last time I slept for a full night with no interruptions.

"What's the plan for the day?" I ask around a mouthful of pastry.

"We can have a beach day and get to know one another more if you'd like. Do you like to read? Watch television? What's a hobby for you?"

I swallow a gulp of coffee. "I like to read."

Colby grins at me. "Yeah? Me too. What's your favorite genre?"

"Classics. I frequently dabble in romance, science fiction, and fantasy though."

Colby blinks at me, another one of those looks on his face like he's trying to figure me out. "We can take a run into town to the bookstore unless you brought some books with you?"

*Yes, I brought books for what I thought was going to be a fuck fest*, I want to say but don't. Instead, I just smile at him warmly.

"A trip to the bookstore would be great. I'm sure I can knock a few books out if we just mostly relax on the beach."

"We'll go before we hit the beach so you have a book for today."

Once I'm done eating, Colby takes the tray and leaves the bedroom without so much as a word. I roll out of bed, then softly pad to the bathroom. Blinking away the rest of the sleep from my eyes, I stretch and pull off the shirt Colby slipped on me last night. I inspect the shirt for a moment, wondering if it holds any keys to Colby Smith. It reads "Clay Road Farms" with pictures of trees against a dark teal shirt. Maybe it's a business from wherever he lives?

Carefully, I fold the shirt, laying it on the white granite bathroom counter. I turn the shower on, patiently waiting for it to heat up. The door pushes open just after I finish brushing my teeth. Colby meets my eyes in the mirror with a heated look.

"Can I join you in the shower?"

Oh, hell yeah. "Of course, husband."

He sighs deeply and closes his eyes. An odd look of pain crosses his face but it disappears just as quickly as it appeared. If I didn't know better, I'd think I had imagined it. I step into the shower with a blissful moan. The showerhead rains hot water over me, quickly steaming the bathroom up despite the sun rays shining through the windows. Just as I'm starting to shampoo my hair, Colby joins me.

My eyes fall to his cock out of sheer habit. Jesus Christ. He has the biggest cock I've ever seen. The prettiest one too. It's long, girthy, and he's so hard that it curves towards his stomach. I swallow and meet his heated gaze. I rinse the shampoo out of my hair, then step backward, out of the spray of water. He follows me until he's pressing me against the cold tiled wall.

A hiss escapes me at the sharp sting of the cold tile

against my back but it quickly turns into a moan when his hand slowly glides up my thigh, to my hip, and under my belly button, teasing me, not yet putting his hand where I really want it. I bite my lip, blinking up at him, begging him with my eyes to touch me. To put me out of my misery.

He takes mercy on me and finally wraps his broad hand around my cock.

"This is mine for the week," he says firmly, without any pretense.

"Yeah," I confirm with a breathy moan.

Colby crowds into me further until his cock is pressed against my stomach. His hand holds me firmly, hand trapped between our stomachs, and dips down to bite my lower lip. I tremble in need against him.

"What do you want, Eli?"

I blink hazily up at him. "What do you mean?"

"What do you want?" Colby repeats, his thumb now lazily circling the head of my cock. I almost fall to my knees under his spell. "You want me to get on my knees in the shower and suck you off? You want me to turn you around, shove you against the wall, and eat you out until you're trembling and begging for it? You want me to jerk you off so that you get your cum all over me? What do you want?"

Oh, Jesus Christ. I stare up at him, panting, astounded at my inability to just fucking answer him. It's easy, Eli. Just open your mouth and tell him what you want. Instead, I stare at him like a fish with my mouth open, chest heaving with desire. He chuckles, the sound rough and low. Colby slides his hand down my cock once, before sliding back up to repeat circling his thumb around the head.

What is this magic he's working over me? It's been one day.

"Like this, then," he whispers before taking my mouth in a harsh kiss. He kisses me so hard that it's difficult for me to get air. But I like it. His hand on my cock is borderline painful, the grip almost too tight, but every swipe of his thumb over the head has me seeing galaxies behind my closed eyes.

When he grabs my thigh and hitches it up to his waist, I come. Without absolutely any warning. I gasp against his mouth, whimper too, and let him eat at my mouth until I'm trembling from the oversensitivity of his hand on my spent cock. He lets me go with a chuckle. My heart races as I watch him use his cum-covered hand to wrap around his own rigid cock.

My legs go weak at the sight. No one has ever done that with me before. I stare transfixed as he works his cock over using only my cum as lube. His other hand reaches up to my neck, his thumb pressing my chin up so that I have to meet his fathomless gaze. I watch as his lips part on a moan, and he grips my jaw tight, eyes on me.

"Tell me you want this," he says, voice wrecked.

"I want this," I tell him truthfully. I want him to let go and treat me like all I mean to him is sex. That's all this is for a week. Sex.

He lets out one long pained moan before coming all over my stomach. The heat of his release rockets through me, making me close my eyes out of relief. I stand there, frozen, unable to move at all, until the soft caress of a loofah brushes against my skin. My eyes blink open to find him washing me off with his own loofah and body wash.

I get the feeling I'm in for a wild ride this week for which I wasn't properly prepared. The man before me is not what I expected. He is soft and gentle but at other times there's an underlying meanness to him. A dominance that I never knew I craved.

Time will tell if I escape unscathed.

---

THE BOOKSTORE ISN'T FAR from the beach house. Colby's Jeep rumbles down the coastal highway and I feel free sitting beside him. With the top off the Jeep, the wind whips through my hair, no doubt making my curls unmanageable and messy. The car is a manual, so I spend most of my time watching Colby change gears. It's kind of sexy. That's a lie. It's *really* sexy watching a hot man use the stick shift.

After he parks the car in a small lot by the beach, he hops out and runs over to eagerly open my door for me. With a hopeful grin, he holds his hand out to help me climb out of the Jeep. His hand is warm and large, easily enveloping my own, and he doesn't let go even as we cross the street to the bookstore.

Colby ushers me into the quaint beachside bookstore with a possessive hand on the small of my back. This man definitely likes to touch and he doesn't care if anyone in this town sees. He abruptly stops at the entrance of the store.

Colby gestures for me to peruse the store. "Anything you want, it's yours."

I take his hand into my own and start down one of the aisles. He's a quiet presence beside me as I look through the small selection in the store. I grab a new fantasy novel I've been meaning to read and hand it to Colby. We go up and down the aisles like that until he can no longer hold my hand due to having such a large stack of books.

"You'll read these all in a week?" he questions me, a frown on his beautiful face.

I shrug effortlessly. "I'm a fast reader."

He follows me into the children's section with an even more confused look on his face. "What are we looking for in this section?"

"You'll see," I tell him with a teasing smile.

I always look for a certain book in bookstores. My mother loves *The Wind in the Willows* and I always grab a copy when I see it. I let out a triumphant whoop when I find a copy on the bottom shelf, tucked away in the corner. It's a gorgeous version, with an illustrated sleeve, and a deep lilac hardcover. Neither of us has this one yet. A total win.

"What's that?"

I hold it out to him. "*The Wind in the Willows.*"

"Never read it," Colby says, taking a closer look at the cover.

"Ah," I sigh softly. "It's one of my absolute favorites. I have this thing with my mom where I buy a copy whenever I see it and send a picture to her so she knows I'm thinking about her. She does the same thing."

Colby beams down at me. "I love that."

I add the book to the precarious stack in his hands and nod towards the register. "Alright, husband, time to make the purchase."

He makes a show of carrying the stack to the register. The girl at the counter rings them up with a smile at us.

"Planning to get a lot of reading done on your vacation?" she asks conversationally while popping a bubble of gum.

"If I let him," Colby tells her before I can even attempt to answer.

I notice for the first time that there's a tan line on his

finger where a wedding band would've rested. I wonder if he's married and this is an escape for him. It's not quite my business, I'm being paid, but I always hate the idea of someone cheating with me. I never want to cause someone that type of pain. It's not my business though, so I won't ask. I glance away from his hand just in time to avoid being caught. He smiles at me as he pays, then takes the heavy canvas bag from the cashier.

"Should we get lunch in town?"

I look towards the restaurants, then back over my shoulder. "Let's go back to the house. I'd rather spend the day alone with you on the beach."

That clearly makes him happy because he aims a pleased-as-punch grin my way. On the way back to the beach house he turns the radio on, some rock station with songs from when I was a kid echoing through the speakers. I watch as his fingers tap the tune against the steering wheel. He pulls into the garage of the beach house, grabs the books, and comes around to open my door again.

"Colby," I say as I take his hand but don't get out of the Jeep.

"Yeah?"

"You don't have to do this," I whisper into the dark of the garage.

He cocks his head again, scrutinizing me. "Do what?"

I make a helpless gesture towards the books. "I'm an easy thing."

Colby grunts in annoyed frustration. "We talked about this already. I thought we were on the same page."

"Well, even if you were my real husband, I'd say the same thing."

"And if you were my real husband, I'd buy you whatever

*The Husband Experience*

your heart desired so that you always knew you were loved."

I try to hold back my visible flinch. It's a lovely sentiment but one I don't need. We've already had an argument about this, so I hold my tongue. I follow Colby into the house and into the living room where he lays out the books on the coffee table.

"What will you read first?" he asks me eagerly.

I point at the fantasy novel that's about eight hundred pages thick. "Probably that one."

"Alright. Want to head out to the beach?"

"One thing first."

The copy of *Wind in the Willows* really is beautiful. I position it on the table so it's alone and snap a quick photo.

> thinking of you mama

**MAMA**
> love you my sweet boy

> where are you this week?

> Florida. I'm playing boyfriends.

**MAMA**
> be safe.

> always! love you!

**MAMA**
> love you too

. . .

I SMILE down at my phone for a moment, then glance up to find Colby watching me.

"Beach time?"

"Yeah," Colby replies softly.

We change into our swimsuits and I follow along behind Colby out to the private beach. He lays out a large beach towel that'll fit both of us.

After getting comfortable on my stomach, I open the book up to start reading. Colby lies down beside me, sunglasses over his eyes, and happily stares up at the sky. I try to read, I really do, but I can't concentrate with Colby beside me. Not with all the thoughts running through my brain. I keep trying to read for almost thirty minutes but give up with a frustrated huff.

"Not good?" Colby asks, head angled my way.

"I got three pages in the past thirty minutes."

"So ... that's bad, right?"

"I can't concentrate."

"Why?"

I huff again and move to straddle him. "I didn't come here to read."

I press my hands into his chest, feeling the coarse hairs there. He feels wonderful between my thighs, powerful and strong. My heart kicks a crazy beat up in my chest when he moves a little, so I can feel his cock filling underneath me. That's more like it.

Colby pushes his sunglasses up his face with one finger. "Maybe relaxing isn't up your alley. We can go deep sea fishing or catamaraning. We can do a dolphin sighting tour or go paddleboarding."

I leer down at him, baring my teeth. "I didn't come here for any of that either."

Colby reaches up to sweetly brush a wayward curl from my forehead. "You're not going to calm down until I've fucked you, are you?"

I bite my lip, intoxicated just by the idea of it. "Definitely not. So will you?"

He nods against the blanket, a flush darkening his cheeks. "Yeah, tonight. Can you wait that long?"

I stare down at him, frustrated and deeply annoyed. He definitely likes making me wait. I'm beginning to wonder what exactly Colby Smith is planning to do with me. Patience is not my strongest virtue.

"Fine," I say between gritted teeth.

He just smiles serenely up at me. "It'll be worth the wait. I promise."

Yeah, whatever. I roll off him and stare up at the sky in annoyance. A few birds fly overhead as the clouds block the sun. Colby better be the best fuck of my life to make me wait so long. Like what kind of john doesn't fuck his paid piece the minute he walks through the door? Oh, husband, blah blah blah. Whatever.

Colby leans up on his elbows, blocking the cloudless sky from my view.

"Are you sulking?" Colby asks around a teasing smile.

"No," I grit out.

"Hmm." He brushes his mouth gently over mine and tugs on one of my curls. "Get in the water with me?"

He helps me stand and I follow him out into the ocean like a lost puppy. I just barely resist the urge to stomp my feet in the sand.

# 3

## COLBY

Eli Ruiz is going to ruin me. Just like last night, he's sulky through most of dinner. A glass of wine seems to do the trick of relaxing him, so I give him another tonight. Miraculously it works again. He sips at the moscato, head tilted back to look up at the darkening sky, and I wonder what's going through his brain.

Is he wondering why a forty-year-old man has purchased his pleasure for a week? Is he wondering why I brought him to my beach house? Is he wondering what I'm going to be like in bed? I don't know what he's thinking but I wish I knew. It's been so long since I let myself get lost in somebody.

Marcus died three years ago from pancreatic cancer. He never even made it to see a year after fifty. It took me a while to get him to settle down with me, but he was worth the wait. Marcus was my wild child despite being older than me. He tested me in every way, made me better, made me want for things I had never wanted before. I miss him every single day.

But I have to move on, for myself and for his memory. I'm

ready to love again, to take care of someone, to have a partner.

Maybe I can break past that barrier inside me that says I can never have something like what I had with Marcus again. Beau used The Boyfriend Experience and had nothing but great things to say. Something about this experience has to help me, get me over the divide I've been so afraid to jump.

The problem is Eli. I can't figure him out. Yeah, he's here to play my boyfriend but I don't want a totally contrived experience. I want to be with a person this next week, not a robot. So I need to shatter through his barriers to get him to relax. If fucking him will get him to relax, that's not a hardship on my end.

He's beautiful with dark, curly hair, long eyelashes, a few moles scattered around his lithe torso, and eyes that penetrate me to the very depths of my soul.

Eli finishes his wine, then carefully sets the empty glass on the table. He blinks his dark brown eyes at me a few times and smiles in a way that sets my blood to boiling. He's got a gorgeous damn smile with wide lips that are made to be kissed, made to be bruised from my teeth biting down on them.

"Will you take me to bed now, husband?" Eli asks, voice low and husky, just the right side of wicked too.

I don't bother cleaning up the table, which is highly unusual for me. I like cleanliness and order in most aspects of my life. Eli lets out a surprised gasp when I pull him out of his seat. He sways for a second, but I steady him with a firm grip on his waist.

"Go ahead of me and get ready," I order him, nodding towards the stairs.

He blinks slowly again, eyes focusing back on me, before

*The Husband Experience*

biting his lip and worrying the tender flesh a little between his teeth. With a nod, he tugs out of my grip and heads towards the bedroom with a purposeful stride. My watch says it's just shy of six in the evening, so I stand and stare at the ocean as I give him a fifteen-minute head start. The sun is at just the right angle to be sending an orange glow over the water as the waves break against the shore.

I watch the seagulls fly above the beach for a while, letting myself get distracted. I try not to think about this being the first time I've fucked someone that isn't Marcus since my twenties. If I think about it too much, I might not be able to go through with it.

Once fifteen minutes creep slowly by, I head into the house, and up to the bedroom. The image that greets me takes my breath away, like a punch to my chest. I open the door to find Eli spread out on the bed, knees bent, putting on a filthy show for me.

"Fuck," I say out loud. I don't think my cock has ever hardened so fast. Just from the sight of him. Sweaty and waiting for me on the bed, his lip caught between his teeth.

"I couldn't wait," he whimpers as he glides a lube-slicked hand up and down his cock. "But I didn't finish prepping myself because you said you want to do that." Eli huffs a little as his hips thrust up into the tight grip of his fingers. "Please get over here. Please touch me."

His breathy plea goes straight to my cock. Every single ounce of control in my body snaps. I hurriedly hop around to remove my pants, underwear, and then finally my shirt. A relieved sigh escapes him when I join him on the bed, letting our naked skin finally touch.

His hair is messy from the day, but also from his head

dipping back on the pillow in pleasure. The tight corkscrew curls hide half of his lust-blown gaze from me.

Running my hands up his thighs, I pull them further apart so that I can fit myself between them. For a while I sit there and just watch him touch himself.

His cock isn't particularly big, but it's nice sized, and I liked the feel of it in my hand this morning. I know I'll like the feel of it in my mouth too. The idea of sucking him has me clenching my jaw with want. My mouth practically waters at the idea of it weighty and swollen against my tongue. Fuck.

"Stop touching yourself," I demand, voice husky.

Eli lets out a little whimper but stops. He pants as he stares up at me from under his eyelashes. I grab the lube from beside him, pouring a generous amount onto my fingers.

"Flip over." I use my hand to help guide Eli onto his knees, then I spread his gorgeous cheeks. God. I can't wait to be inside him. I rub lube over his hole, gently pressing a finger in, teasing him just a little. He's so fucking tight. A little gasp escapes Eli at my touch. I can tell that he's trying to keep me from hearing his sounds.

"Let me hear you and don't lie to me. If something hurts, tell me. If you want me to stop, tell me. If you want me to do more of something, tell me too. You have to tell me what you want."

Eli lets out a frustrated noise. "What I want is for you to stop talking, get lube inside me, and then fuck me. That's what I want."

I slap his ass once and smile at his pleased inhale. I do as he says though because I know not everyone is a fan of lengthy prep. Once I'm done getting him ready, I put a condom on, slick myself up, and kneel behind him. I run a hand up his bare back, feeling the bumps of his spine beneath my broad palm. He's not a tiny man but he's on the thinner side, easily eclipsed by my larger body.

I slowly push into him, watching as I disappear into the tight vise of his body. He takes me easily, as if he was made for me, and I try to not think about that too much. I take a steadying breath once I'm fully inside, my hips flush against his ass. I stay there for a moment so he can adjust, but again, I've underestimated him. Eli shoves back against me with another annoyed grunt.

"Come on, Colby." There's an edge of petulance to his voice that calls to something inside me that I haven't thought about for years. "Please," he says even more softly as his fingers tangle in the rumpled bedsheets.

I take mercy on him and start to move. The glow of sunset fills the room, turning Eli's sweat-slick skin a beautiful shade of burnt orange. His enthusiastic moans, my breathless whines, and the sound of our skin meeting ... it's more than I can bear. It's been too long since I've been with someone like this, since I've felt the thrill of having someone underneath me. Giving someone pleasure while taking my own.

I tug him up until his back is pressed to my chest, so we're both on our knees. I can reach my hand around his neck perfectly. His face is gorgeous from this angle, his parted lips, and firmly shut eyes, he's so fucking beautiful. Turning his face as I continue to thrust deeply inside him, I press my mouth to his parted lips. He moans into my mouth as I thrust into him even sharper, nailing the spot inside him that makes him see stars, and that's when I've got his number.

My Eli likes it just on the edge of pain. But I think maybe he might like something else more.

"We'll talk about this later," I whisper against Eli's sweat-slicked cheek.

"Whatever," he numbles before letting out a moan when I roughly slap his thigh.

"You're a bad, bad boy."

He nods fervently against my shoulder. "So bad."

"But you'll be good for me, right? You can be my good boy."

Eli lets out a stifled cry. His thighs quake and his lips tremble in need against my own. Oh, he likes that too. I wonder how often he gets called a good boy, how often he gets praised. I will make it my mission the next few days to make it just a tad rough, but tell him how good he is too. A beautiful dichotomy.

I bite his neck hard as I reach down to take his cock in my hand. I can feel the rising tension in his body, feel that he's close to the edge, and I decide to not tease him tonight. I'll get him there fast and let him come. Because I'm a nice guy. I speed up, gritting my teeth against my own impending orgasm, and tug harder on his cock.

He tenses against me and goes limp as he comes into my hand with a muffled shout. I know not everyone likes to be fucked after they come, so I pull out and roughly shove him onto the bed. He goes happily, blinking up at me in the dazed way that makes me feel decidedly possessive. Leaning over him, I take off the condom to tug rapidly at my cock.

"Yeah," Eli eggs me on while biting his lip. "Come all over me. I'll sleep with it on me. I'll wear you on my skin so everyone knows I'm yours. I'm yours. Aren't I, husband?"

I come with a groan, painting his taut stomach with my release. He grins up at me, head cocked to the side, curls askew and damp with sweat. I watch, entranced, as he swipes a finger through the cum on his stomach to bring it to his mouth. He sucks the cum off, then releases his finger with a loud smacking pop.

If my dick could rally, it would. I lean down and kiss him, swiping my tongue into his mouth to taste my release mixed with the taste of Eli. A small, happy moan escapes him and I swallow it down. I lean over to grab my T-shirt, but when I return to wipe Eli off, he shakes his head at me.

"I'm wearing it."

A shocked laugh bursts out of me. "You can't be serious. That'll be so uncomfortable."

"Fine," Eli relents. "But leave a little on me and rub it in."

I do as he asked. I wipe most of it off but leave a little, then gently rub it into his skin. He closes his eyes with a blissful smile on his face. I kiss him once more before tossing the shirt to the floor. The mess will bother me but it's worth it to lie beside Eli post-orgasm. He curls up in my arms, satiated and smelling like me, and I think that maybe this wasn't the worst decision I've ever made. Actually, I think it's pretty far from it.

He rubs his cheek against my chest like a cat, so I play with the curls on top of his head. It's still early, the sun just now dipping below the horizon, but only a few moments go by before I hear Eli letting out soft snores. I lie awake for a while, just running my fingers through his hair, listening to the sweet sounds he makes in his sleep.

I'm going to figure Eli out if it's the last thing I do. This week can be as much for him as it is for me. I'll see to that.

---

ELI MOVING RESTLESSLY beside me wakes me up from my own fitful sleep. Indecipherable mutters escape him while he twitches helplessly on the other side of the bed. The sun isn't even up yet. I roll across the bed, sling an arm across his waist, and tug him against me.

He stills, mumbling something I still can't understand, then snuggles back against me. I assume he's gone back to sleep, but he proves me wrong.

"Sorry," he mumbles softly.

"It's fine," I reassure him, rubbing my thumb against his hip. "I was sleeping badly myself. You okay?"

He hums dismissively. A moment goes by before he tugs my hand with his own, wrapping it around his chest. I bury my face in his messy curls and brush my lips against the sweaty nape of his neck. A shiver passes through him, so I pull him tight against me, seeking my own comfort in his still sleep-slack body.

"I've always talked in my sleep," Eli explains, words still a little sleep slurred. "Since I was a kid. If it'll bother you, then I can sleep in another bedroom."

"No," I whisper roughly against his neck. "We'll sleep together this week."

I'd missed having someone else in the bed with me. I don't care if he talks in his sleep, walks in his sleep, or even elbows me nonstop... we will sleep in the same bed for the next few nights. I know it'll be hard when I return home but I'll deal with it then.

"Think you can fall back asleep or are you up?"

He lets out a jaw-cracking yawn. "Sadly I'm up. Once I wake up, I can't go back to sleep. Unless I'm sick. Then I can nap or fall back asleep during the night."

I chuckle against his neck. "Good to know."

He stills in my arms. Just when I'm about to ask him what I've said, he rolls over to face me in the dark. Even with only the light of the moon in the bedroom, he's a beautiful thing. His eyes are so big, like doe eyes. Big and searching me for answers I don't know how to give.

"Well, if we're both awake." He cuddles up close to me, blinking those big eyes at me. I can't help but let out a chuckle. His eyes narrow at me in agitation, and he goes to roll away, but I hold him tight, unwilling to let go.

"How about we talk instead."

"Yes," Eli drawls with an eye roll, "we're husbands for the week to talk."

"That's what husbands do," I tell him, landing a soft smack on his ass. "They talk. Husbands don't just fuck all the time."

"Fine," Eli relents.

"Let's talk about our limits."

Eli grunts. "Sure. I have basically no limits. I mean I have soft limits, but you paid fifty thousand dollars for me, so for that price, there are no limits."

"Well, we're not doing golden showers or scat or blood play. Right off the bat."

He blinks those big eyes at me again. "Fine. But just so you know, those are my favorite things, so this entire experience has soured for me."

I let out a loud laugh and he grins wickedly back at me. "Touché."

Throwing his leg over my hip, he plays with my hair. I close my eyes against the touch, luxuriating in the simple act of being touched for no other reason than being touched. It's been so long. Eli's touch is so tender, so gentle, as if he knows I've been without it for far too long. His fingers scratch at my hair, before soothing the skin, and then trailing softly along the back of my neck.

"Go on," Eli urges softly.

"How do you feel about being dominated?"

"Love it."

"Spanked?"

"A plus."

"Choked?"

"If you've got experience with breath play, then sure."

"Biting?"

Eli bites his lip. I feel him start to grow hard against me. "Yep."

"Edging?" I ask, voice low and husky.

Eli shrugs. "I can take it or leave it but it really depends on the partner."

I run my nose along his cheek and kiss his forehead. His fingers dig into my scalp for a moment before relaxing. I use this as my chance to kiss down to his neck, to his throat, then nip at his Adam's apple. His leg tightens around my waist for a moment as he ruts against me.

"Primal play?" I ask, my voice a low growl. I shiver helplessly when his cock leaves a trail of pre-cum on the skin of my stomach.

"Fuck," Eli whispers hoarsely just before pressing his mouth roughly against mine.

I gently roll him onto his back, kissing him deep and slow. Licking into his mouth, tasting him, it's easily one of the top-five kisses of my entire life. Eli lets out these little moans as we kiss that I fervently wish I could record and play back later when I need them most. I pull away to lean on my forearms, hovering above him. Despite the darkness of the room,

I can easily see the visible flush high on his cheeks. Desire shimmers in his hooded eyes.

Rolling my hips against him, I slide our cocks together until he's shivering beneath me. It's a little dry without lube, so I hold my hand in front of him, and without even needing to ask, he licks a wet stripe up my palm. Quickly, I take both of our cocks in hand and start rutting. It only takes a moment before he's coming, legs tight around my waist, and I use his cum like I did in the shower to finish myself off.

I'm not letting him lie around covered in my cum again. I grab some tissues and wipe us both down. He laughs in the dark, a breathy little laugh, and softly kisses the corner of my mouth in thanks.

"I've never been chased and fucked before but I'd say that was an enthusiastic yes to trying that one out," he says sweetly, still a little out of breath.

I kiss him once more with my own smile. After a few sweet, orgasm-soft kisses, I tug him out of the bed to shower together. Under the rainfall shower, I tenderly wash him, skimming my fingers over the soft skin of his abdomen. His stomach contracts under my fingers and he hisses at my touch. I kiss him again because I can, because I want to, because his kisses are rapidly becoming one of my favorite pastimes. We kiss so long that the water runs cold, something that's never happened here before. I try to not dwell on that too much as we start our day.

# 4
## ELI

Colby makes me breakfast again but this time we don't eat it in bed. The sky changes from a dark blue to light blues and purples as I sit at the large kitchen island. Every single molecule in my body is relaxed, despite my mind constantly telling me I should be on guard. Colby slides a plate of over-hard eggs towards me, with a bagel, and some cut-up fruit because he's actually an angel.

I wrinkle my nose in distaste at the fruit though. "Thank you."

He laughs at me, a dimple popping out under his beard. "Got a problem with blueberries?"

I get to work slathering butter on the bagel, pile the egg on, and grab the hot sauce he sets in front of me. Good to go. After I take a bite, moaning through it of course, I look back at him to find him staring at me with mild concern.

"Oh sorry. Yeah, I don't like any kind of berry ..."

He has the gall to look disgruntled. "I'm sorry, what?"

"I don't like berries," I repeat carefully.

"What do you mean you don't like berries?" he asks, voice

contrite and mildly angry. I love getting this reaction from people.

"I don't like how they're not predictable. Sometimes they're sour ... sometimes they're mushy ... sometimes they're sweet. If they were the same every time, they'd be awesome."

He tilts his head at me like a golden retriever, which I'm noticing is a thing he often does towards me.

"Strawberries though?"

"Well, I'm allergic to strawberries, so that's different."

"So different," Colby replies with an eye roll. "Not all fruit though?"

"I love apples and bananas and pineapple and kiwi and grapes—"

"I get it," Colby interrupts me with a deep laugh.

I watch through narrowed eyes as he plates himself an over-easy egg and some bread to dip into it. A good selection of fruit covers his plate, but I'm not very surprised. Something about Colby screams *he takes care of himself* to me. Mostly because his body is still in amazing shape for a man his age.

He's got abs, even though they're not super defined, but he's still got a magnificent body. Colby has the type of body built for strength, not for show. I really like his biceps. Every time he moves his arms, the muscles pop out, tight and firm. I bet he could hold me up for hours while he fucks me against a wall.

I sigh at the image that gives me.

"What?" Colby asks around a mouthful of food.

I wrinkle my nose. "Nothing."

We eat the rest of breakfast in silence as the sun rises higher in the sky.

Not for the first time, I wonder why Colby felt the need to

hire me. To hire a sex worker at all. I've done this enough to know that people have many different reasons. Some like sex a certain way and are afraid to have a relationship because of it. Some people like the dynamic of purchasing me, of knowing I can say no but it'll be a hard-fought line to get there. Some people are shy and it's the only way they can enjoy intimacy. Colby Smith is none of those things.

I help Colby clean up breakfast by rinsing the dishes once he washes them. The man still puts them in the dishwasher though, even after they've been thoroughly washed by us. Not worth commenting on because we've all got our quirks.

"Do you want to relax today or take another journey into town?" Colby asks as he watches me walk around the living room.

A white baby grand piano sits at the edge of the living room, facing the ocean. I wonder if Colby plays, but I mostly wonder if I can goad him into fucking me against the piano. Maybe I can scratch a few things off my sexual bucket list this week if I play my cards right.

"Whatever you want to do," I tell him while trailing my fingers along the piano.

His eyes are heavy on me from across the room, so I decide to put on a show. In just my boxer briefs, with the soft morning sun streaming through the windows, I lean against the piano in the lewdest way possible.

"Eli," Colby reprimands, voice husky.

"Yes?" I blink coyly at him over my shoulder, wiggling my ass a little in invitation.

Colby takes a step closer, but stops out of reach. "What do you want to do today?"

"You know, I have always wanted to get fucked against a piano. It's very *Pretty Woman* of me, I think. My darling husband railing me against a piano sounds like the best way to start my day."

Colby takes the last few steps to cross the room, stride purposeful and eyes boring into me. He presses against me, the solid line of his chest firm against my back. I hold back a moan at the feel of his hard cock against my ass. God, yes.

"Eli," Colby whispers against my ear, hands tight against my hips. "Stop goading me on. We're leaving the house today. I'll fuck you however you want tonight, but you'll have to wait."

I let my head fall with a clunk against the piano as he steps away from me, taking his heat with him. The asshole just chuckles softly behind me.

"I like edging in the bedroom only. Are you going to edge me all day?" I ask, clearly irritated.

When I turn around, his eyes are heavy on me, running down my body like a caress.

"You're a brat."

I blink at him. "Do you like it?"

Colby grunts, lips twitching in barely restrained amusement. "Obviously. Are you always like this?"

I flush and look away from him. "No."

"Just for your husband?"

God, Colby is going to kill me. I nod, unable to form words. Colby crosses the distance between us again to wrap me in his arms. He kisses me, soft and sweet, and tastes like blueberries. I don't mind the flavor so much when it's on his tongue.

My body relaxes against him as his large hands splay against my shoulder blades, pulling me closer against his warm body. Kisses have never been my favorite thing but kissing Colby Smith is slowly becoming addicting. The way he licks into my mouth, owning me with his lips, settles something in my perpetually impatient soul.

I'm dazed and starry-eyed when he finally pulls away. Colby pushes some of my wayward curls away from my forehead with a tender smile. I love the way his eyes crinkle at the corner when he smiles—so soft, so startlingly sweet.

"Be good today and I'll give you anything you want tonight. Think you can do that?" I nod eagerly and he grins at me. "Such a good boy."

I suck in an inhale because suddenly I'm dizzy. I've had a lot of encounters over the years, paid for and just for my pleasure. But no one has found my praise kink as quickly as Colby. Most times people seem more into degradation than anything, which is not remotely one of my kinks. Sure, I'll perform, but it does nothing for me.

Being told I'm a good boy? Well, that lights up all the happy little nerve endings throughout my entire body. Colby just chuckles at my dazed expression and tugs me towards the bedroom by the hand.

"I've got a surprise for you," Colby tells me once we're finished getting dressed. He's wearing board shorts, an old faded T-shirt, and a black ball cap. Although he had a slight beard when I arrived, he's not shaved since, so it's messy and wiry, and I like it. The man always looks effortlessly good.

"Oh yeah?"

I follow him out of the house and into the Jeep. He loads a cooler into the Jeep along with a canvas bag of supplies. Colby puts a hand on my knee as we pull out of the driveway and set off for the surprise destination. I remind myself to not get used to this treatment. This is an act, we're playing husbands, no one else will likely ever treat me this way.

Not because I'm not deserving of it but because it's

doubtful I'll find someone so willing to spoil me like this ever again. It's easy to allow myself to be spoiled under the pretend husband pretense. Something about Colby has made me open up in a way that previous experiences haven't.

The Jeep speeds along the coastal highway for just long enough for me to get my fix of watching Colby drive. Colby pulls into a small but crowded marina. He uses a swipe card to admit us through the gate, navigating the Jeep towards a private parking lot that hugs the water.

I wait for him to hop out and open my door because I'm learning that Colby likes that. He takes pleasure in doting on me even if it's hard for me to accept, to allow. He helps me to the ground. A gentle kiss is placed on my lips as a reward for waiting.

He holds his hand out, wiggling his fingers in a clear sign for me to take his hand. So I do. The marina is full of expensive boats, ranging from medium to massive. No clouds dot the sky today, so it's a perfect day to be out on the water. Colby comes to a stop at a medium-sized speed boat with the name *Sweet Darlin'* along the side.

The boat rocks gently in the water as we move about. Supple tan leather covers the seating at the end of the boat. I take a seat as Colby bustles around the boat. He rests the cooler by my feet, and dips down to give me a lingering kiss.

"There's an island thirty minutes out that we can explore. I thought you might like that," Colby says as a flush fills out his cheeks.

I smile sweetly, warmed by his gesture. "I love that."

I tug him down to me to kiss him once more. His smile presses into my mouth, tasting like pure sunshine. That's what Colby tastes like, sunshine, joy, and humid summer days.

Wind whips against my face as we work our way out of the marina. Colby looks back at me every now and then, so I smile at him in reassurance. This man is so sweet and caring towards me, the escort he's hired, that I'm a little thrown by it still. I'd expected a week of debauchery, not a week of tender dates and fond kisses.

I attempt to carefully rebuild the wall around my heart as we speed through the turquoise waves. Salt air rushes over me, healing me in ways I hadn't known I needed to be healed. An island appears on the horizon, small but full of palm trees with rocks stemming out from the edges. Colby pulls up to a small wooden dock that's definitely seen better days and ties us to it.

I grab the canvas bag before Colby can argue, following along behind him towards the island. A small hut sits at the edge of the trees and Colby eagerly heads towards it. Placing the cooler on the small wooden table, he gently takes the canvas bag from me.

"I've brought lunch, drinks, snorkeling masks, and sunscreen. Anything we could need for a day at the island."

I cock my head at him. "Is this *your* island?"

He only chuckles at me as he yanks his T-shirt off. I try to not get distracted by the sudden appearance of so much glorious tanned skin. "It belongs to the state park a little ways up the coast, but you need a permit to come out here. It's a weekday, so it should be just us."

"This is lovely, thank you, Colby."

He flushes again before slathering sunscreen on himself, then onto me. I don't have the heart to tell him that I never burn, I'll just tan, because he seems to take such pleasure in the simple act of caring for me. I kiss his stubbled cheek in gratitude once he's done. I walk down to the shore, with him plodding along behind me, and sigh as the water laps at my feet.

"It's the perfect temperature."

"It usually is this time of year."

I tip my head towards the sky, closing my eyes to feel the sun on my skin. God, I could live in this moment forever. A sweet man who wants to fuck me, have me, and the salt air against my skin. We spend the next few hours just basking in the ocean. Colby stays close to me the entire time.

Finally, when I'm starting to prune, we climb out to eat the lunch Colby packed. It's only sandwiches and cut vegetables with dip but it's lovely all the same. He even packed dessert, cookies from a bakery in town.

I take a bite of mine and then kiss him so he can taste it on my lips. "These are good."

"Best bakery in town."

"Take me before I go home?" I ask, but I'm just rewarded with another kiss instead of an answer.

After lunch I amble towards the rocks jutting out of the island. Colby watches me, hawk-eyed, as I carefully step across the rocks. There's a little alcove between the rocks and the sand filled with darker blue water. I see starfish and a few shells inside. It's beautiful. I point it out to Colby with an excited grin over my shoulder.

"Look!" I point out, ecstatic at my find.

Colby bobs in the water a few feet away. "That's so cool, baby."

*Baby.* It must've been a habit because Colby's face shutters closed right after he said it. I'm not an asshole, so I ignore the entire thing, but the endearment was lovely.

After taking one last look at my find, I climb out to the last rock on the edge, diving into the water to swim towards

Colby. Once I'm close enough to him, he reaches out, tugging me to him in the shallows.

I let out a surprised noise when he kisses me hungrily, devouring my mouth with a frenzy he hasn't before. I go boneless against him and let him kiss me, let him eat at my mouth, his fingers almost too tight in my soaking wet curls.

I'm gasping for breath when he pulls away. His pupils are blown wide with desire and I feel him hard against my stomach. Reaching up, I brush my fingers against his dark blond beard. He tilts his face into my palm. Sweet Colby, but there's a sadness underneath his sweetness that calls to me. I want to care for him this week, give him what he needs from me.

Just as we're pulling away in the boat, I snap a photo of the waves, with a hint of the island at the edge.

I shoot the picture off to the boyfriends group chat.

BENJI
WHERE ARE YOU!

TREVOR
Did you not look at his picture?

BENJI
STFU

JACKSON
Stop yelling please, it's unprofessional

BENJI
YOU SHUT UP TOO JACKSON. I JUST WANT TO KNOW WHERE HE IS!

OMG

BENJI

> HELLO?

Colby took me to a private island today. We're going home now.

JACKSON

> Send a pic of ur sugar daddy

I BITE my lip and take a secret picture of Colby at the wheel, his bare back to the camera, all muscle and a slight sunburn. Before I can talk myself out of it, I send the picture to the boyfriend group chat.

BENJI

> omg....... Wow very happy for you eye roll

TREVOR

> Be careful

BENJI

> Wet blanket Trevor

TREVOR

> Okay sunshine

BENJI

> I'll kill you

JACKSON

> Don't admit that in a text chain

> Miss you guys

BENJI

> Invite us to the wedding!!!!!!!

TREVOR

> You watch pretty woman too much

JACKSON

> Okay, everyone break!

I SLYLY TUCK my phone back into the canvas bag. I've known Jackson the longest, having been with the agency since undergrad. It might sound weird to say but they're kind of all my best friends. We understand each other in a way that other people can't understand us. There's an inherent judgment to doing what we do, even though there shouldn't be.

"You're thinking pretty loudly back there!" Colby shouts over the sound of the engine and the water.

"Just thinking about you!" I yell back.

Colby aims a gorgeous grin over his shoulder that sends my heart rioting in my chest. He slowly guides the boat back into the safety of the marina. I'm exhausted by the time we climb out and make our way towards the Jeep.

"Let's pick dinner up on the way home so you don't have to cook tonight," I say after we buckle in.

Colby turns a tired smile towards me. "You sure? I like cooking."

"Yes, we had a long day. Anything good around here?"

"There's a barbeque place a few minutes from here."

"Let's get that, then."

I twine my fingers with Colby's against his thigh as we make the drive back into town. We stop at the barbeque joint, grabbing enough food to give us leftovers, before finishing the drive back to the beach house. I help Colby unload the vehicle by carrying the food inside. Colby takes the food from me with a thankful smile and puts it into the oven.

He turns to me in the kitchen, skewering me with a look I can't decipher.

Colby takes a steadying deep breath. "I want to take a shower with you, then eat you out against the piano."

Jesus Christ. I let out a little whimper, nodding my agreement. Butterflies fill my stomach as we shower together. I let Colby tenderly wash the sea off of me, the loofah light against my skin. His fingers skim along my skin, making me achingly hard before the shower is even over. I stop him with a hand on his arm as he goes to wash himself, he only raises his eyebrows at me in question. I want to take care of him too. Make him feel even half of what he's making me feel.

I gingerly take the loofah from him, proceeding to tenderly wash his body. The soap bubbles along his strong stomach, the bunched muscles of his back, and those biceps that could crush me if I let them. I pull him under the water with me and kiss him gently, just a tender press of lips without tongue. His hands tighten against my hips, fingertips digging almost painfully into my skin, before letting go so we can climb out and dry off.

Colby leads me naked to the piano and carefully situates me against it. Sizzling excitement fills the air between us. He drags the bench behind me, puts my left foot up on it, then places an openmouthed kiss to the center of my back. I feel myself flush because I'm so open to him in this position.

Rimming isn't my favorite thing. Sure, it's happened, but most of the time I'm doing the rimming. Most people don't focus their experience on my pleasure.

Colby places a trail of wet kisses down my spine causing goosepimples to break out across my skin. The sensations coursing through me are too much. I bite back a whimper as his lips linger just out of reach of where I really want them. My fingers bite painfully into the piano as moans of sheer pleasure get caught in my throat.

His beard scratches against my skin in the most delicious way. A deep shiver rolls through my body when his large hands bracket my hips, lifting me up a little more so I'm spread further apart for him. So he can see all of me.

"So beautiful," Colby murmurs against the cleft of my ass. His breath is wickedly hot on my skin. "You are going to taste divine."

And then his tongue circles my hole. I mewl loudly, scrambling for grip against the piano. My eyes roll back in my head at the sheer, intense ecstasy of it. Every nerve ending inside me lights up as his tongue licks my rim, dipping in to taste. A flush spreads over me, warming me in a way that terrifies me. It's all too much. To top it all off, a deep moan rattles out of him just from the taste of me.

"Colby," I whine breathlessly as his tongue continues to take me apart.

He leans back, spreads my ass cheeks, then lewdly spits on my hole. I gasp. The tip of his thumb dips past my rim, shoving his spit inside. All the air rushes out of me. Jesus. My dick is so hard that I'm afraid if he doesn't touch me, I'll die.

He dives back in like I'm the best meal he's ever eaten.

The hairs of his beard scratch at my skin, but I love every moment of it. I want to have a beard burn on my ass for days. My hearing goes in and out as every ounce of awareness narrows in on where his tongue touches my most intimate place. When my hearing comes back, it's to the sound of a condom wrapper and the snick of the lube bottle.

Thank fuck.

A firm hand presses my chest to lie flat against the piano. I let myself be manhandled until Colby has me exactly how he wants me. I'm just a puppet for his pleasure. My mouth opens on a gasp as Colby pushes in, hard steel into my heat. The glossy sheen of the piano steams up from my rapid pants against it.

Fingers dig into the meat of my hips as he starts a brutal pace so opposite to the tender way he ate me out just moments ago. I hold on for dear life as he fucks me so hard I see stars. Every thrust passes over my prostate, sending tingles throughout my body. I've never been so lit up before just from being fucked. I'm going to come embarrassingly quick.

"Please touch me," I beg as Colby's pace becomes even more frenzied. "Please, husband, touch me. I need you."

"Fuck, Eli," Colby groans against my back, forehead pressed between my shoulder blades. "I should make you wait."

"Noooooooooo," I whine pitifully.

Colby grips my hair and tugs my head back. "You're fucking beautiful like this. Taking me like you were made for me. I want to fuck you for days, keep you like this, begging for my cock."

My legs tremble as I cry out. "I'm not ... Colby ..."

"Call me husband," Colby demands, voice raw and anguished.

"Let me come, husband. Please. I've been so good."

His lube-covered hand wraps tightly around my cock. The firm touch of his hand sends my orgasm detonating through me. I don't even care that I paint the piano with my cum. All I care about is that Colby comes inside me. I fucking need it.

"Come inside me, give it to me. I want to feel you inside me," I beg, my voice sounding wrecked even to my own ears. Colby thrusts so hard that the piano almost shifts beneath us, groaning under the pressure. "Give it to me."

Colby stills deep inside me. I can feel him everywhere. Like he's finally where he belongs. Fear, fresh and painful, grips me just at that fleeting thought. That his body belongs with mine.

He comes with a loud groan against the sweaty nape of my neck. I pant under him, my breath fogging the piano. The setting rays of the sun cast an ethereal glow across the living room as the sound of the waves echoes around us.

We stay there for as long as we can before Colby carefully pulls out of me. I hiss against the loss of him, but try to cover it. The noise must reach him because he returns with a cloth to clean me up, then presses a loving kiss to the small of my spine.

"Did I hurt you?" Colby asks, lips brushing against my overheated skin with each word.

"No," I reply, swallowing every emotion that exists inside me. "Just sensitive."

He hums before turning me around to kiss me. He tastes like both of us mixed together. It's a decadent thing, to taste myself on someone else's tongue. To know my pleasure meant something to them, meant enough for them to keep it on their tongue. I like the taste. A chuckle escapes him when I whine pitifully as he tears away from me.

"Did that fulfill your getting-fucked-against-a-piano wish?"

I laugh lightly. "Yes. I can't feel my legs."

Colby's lips quirk up in a pleased sort of smile. "Stay there."

"As if I could go anywhere without looking like a baby deer."

He chuckles even as he disappears up the stairs. Moments later, he returns with a pair of my boxer briefs and one of his large shirts. He dresses me in his clothes, then picks me up bridal-style. I laugh and hide my face against his neck. He gently sets me down at the kitchen island and proceeds to feed me dinner.

Sun always makes me sleepy, so I'm not surprised that I'm flagging once my stomach is full of the delicious food. Colby cleans up the kitchen and carries me up the stairs to the bedroom. I don't fight him at all. I fall asleep with my back pressed to his chest, the sound of the waves filtering in through the bedroom.

## 5

### COLBY

What am I going to do about Eli? This was supposed to be a week of endless fucking and somehow I have ended up fervently needing to care for him. I want to hold him in his sleep. I want to fuck the brat out of him. Yesterday, when he'd found that small cove by the rocks and grinned widely in excitement over his shoulder at me, my heart had gone into overdrive.

I called him baby.

I *never* even called Marcus baby. Marcus hated endearments, found them off-putting at the best of times. I was Colby and he was Marcus. That was the end of that. And I still loved him until his very final breath because at the end of the day, pet names don't mean anything when you're in a committed relationship. But something about calling Eli baby had just felt right. It felt good.

Eli snuffles sleepily against my chest as I run my fingers through his tight curls. The waves break against the shore outside as the sun fights to rise above the horizon. I know Eli will wake soon, no doubt goading me into fucking him, sucking him, or letting him suck me. But I've missed these sorts of moments the past few years. Just holding someone against me as they sleep. Protecting them. Feeling their warmth seep into me.

Last night against the piano was glorious, borderline akin to heaven. Fucking Eli into submission, making him beg, hearing him ask me to give it to him. I helplessly shiver under the weight of Eli just remembering it.

Eli lets out a soft noise as he curls tighter against my side. I lie there as the sun rises and watch him sleep. An hour or so after the sunrise, his dark brown eyes blink open and gaze up at me. His gaze quickly sharpens at the sight of me watching him. He kisses me softly with a sweet smile tilting his plush lips upwards. I run my hand down his spine to cup one ass cheek in my palm as he tucks his head into my neck with a pleased sigh.

"Are you sore?" I ask, getting a mouthful of curls.

Eli stretches against me, seemingly taking stock of his body. "In a good sort of way."

"Would you like to go dancing tonight?"

Eli lifts his head to look down at me, head cocked. "Dancing?"

I brush curls away from his forehead, grinning when he coyly smirks down at me. "There's a gay nightclub a few towns away. I would like to take you dancing if you want."

"I love to dance," Eli admits with a dreamy sigh. "You wanna show your husband off, huh?"

I grab his hair and tug, making him gasp. "Yeah, I do."

"Wanna show them who I belong to?"

"Yeah."

"I'm your husband," Eli says softly, eyes dipping down to my mouth.

"Husband," I quickly confirm, head dizzy from the word. I take his mouth in a deep kiss. Keeping my hand in his hair, I angle his head until I can kiss him just how I want. "You're such a good boy for me," I murmur against his kiss-slack lips.

"Yeah?" Eli asks dreamily.

I swallow against some emotion I'm too scared to name. "Yeah."

I kiss him once more before rolling out of bed.

Eli lazes in bed as I make him breakfast. When I return with a tray full of waffles, turkey bacon, eggs, and only pineapple, the grin on his face threatens to bring me to my knees.

"Waffles?" Eli asks excitedly. He looks down at the tray in awe before blinking those wide Bambi eyes up at me. "You made waffles for me?"

"Yeah, baby."

Eli flushes bright crimson, then quietly digs into the breakfast. We share off the tray and a few times Eli feeds me, and I happily let him. I nibble at his fingers when he slips a corner of a waffle into my mouth, earning me a beautiful laugh. Eli has the best laugh. It's soft, low, and genuine each time, so I know I've really earned it.

"Can I ask you something?" Eli asks once we've eaten our fill.

I skip my fingers up his spine. "Anything."

Eli glances over at me once before looking out the windows at the horizon. "I noticed a tan line on your finger. I encounter a lot of things being an escort, but my least favorite is when I help someone ruin their marriage. Are you married?"

My hand pauses on his back, and my heart pounds painfully in my chest. Eli can't meet my gaze and I hate it. I hate that even for a moment he's thought I'm that type of man. I'm a lot of things, but that isn't one of them.

"I'm not married," I tell him firmly.

Eli glances back at me. "Yeah?"

"I was married, but I'm not anymore."

Eli takes that as a good enough answer and some of the tension disappears from his shoulders. I tenderly rub my hand up and down his back, feeling the knobs of his spine against my palm. His skin is so warm and golden tan compared to my paler skin. He's only got dark sparse hair on his legs, the rest of him is flawless, golden skin. Except for a nasty scar on his right knee.

"How'd you get that scar?" I ask him, rubbing the scar with my thumb.

Eli hums absentmindedly and kisses my shoulder. "I was in a dirt bike accident as a teenager. Needed surgery on my knee."

"Dirt bike?" I ask in shock.

Eli laughs, rolling his eyes. "I know. I had a crush on an older guy and wanted to be cool. I spent the summer learning to ride a dirt bike at the track. I got pretty good until ... well, my mother wouldn't let me back on track after that."

"Do you get along well with your mother?"

A happy smile forms across Eli's lips. "She's my best friend. She raised me alone and she's a tough chick. She immigrated from Russia as a young girl. My nana was a wonderful woman too. Her favorite phrase was 'tough titties.'"

"I love that." I can't hold back from kissing the hinge of his jaw. "Your dad?"

"She met him on vacation in South America. Had a crazy fling. She told him about me a few months later and he then told her he was married. She gave me his last name just to stick it to him. Sometimes I wish she'd given me her last name. Eli Kozlov sounds pretty good, huh?"

He says everything with a laugh, but I hear it in his voice. The wispiness of his tone, the hard cut of his jaw, it's a soft spot for him. His father. I don't push any further, instead I kiss his closed eyes, then finally his slack mouth. I kiss him down into the bed until he's soft and pliant underneath me. Then I give him the slowest, most decadent blowjob I've ever given, and afterwards I hold him just a little longer than necessary.

---

WE AMBLE DOWN to the shore and spend the afternoon relaxing by the waves.

"I'm gonna get into the water," Eli says sometime later.

I follow after him even though he rolls his eyes at me. I don't like letting him get into the water alone. Not for any particular reason. Ever since Eli walked through those front doors, I've been on high alert for him. One look from him sends the protectiveness inside me careening.

He dips under the warm salt water's surface and breaks back through with a grin. Curls a mess and water dripping down his face, he's so beautiful. I duck down just enough for the water to crash over my shoulders, which Eli finds as an invitation to cling to my back. He adheres to me like a sloth, arms around my shoulders, legs around my waist, face tucked into the crook of my neck.

"Tomorrow's the Fourth of July," Eli mumbles against my neck. He licks me once, making me shiver, before gliding his teeth along my shoulder. "Will there be fireworks?"

I reach back to grip his neck tightly. "Definitely. Do you have another thing on your bucket list?"

"Let's play that one by ear and see if you can figure it out."

"Testing me?"

Eli chuckles, sending vibrations through me. "Just a little."

"I've got your number, Elijah Ruiz."

Eli lets go and swims to face me. "Oh yeah?"

"You're a brat and you like when I take what I want."

A shadow crosses the sun, making it easy for me to see the heat radiate from Eli's eyes just from my words. He launches himself at me, all lips, tongue, and teeth, and I hold him up easily. I skim my hands down his body to cup his ass until he gets the clue and jumps up to wrap his legs around me.

He pulls away panting. "Jesus."

"What was that for?"

"I don't know if this husband shit is working better for you or more for me," Eli admits, butting his forehead against mine.

I can smell the sweetness of him. He smells like the ocean, like something wild and free that I wish so badly to hold on to even after these next few days are over. This is dangerous, but I'm too caught up in him to stop it. Maybe it doesn't have to end. Maybe at the end we can ride into the sunset. *Danger!* My brain screams at me as I carry Eli back on shore. He's not light, but he's not big either, just the perfect size for me to easily handle.

I lay him down on the large beach towel, hovering over him on my forearms.

*The Husband Experience*

"Husband," I whisper to him. A small whimper escapes him.

"Stop," Eli says from between his teeth.

"Why?"

He blinks his hazy brown eyes up at me. "You're going to destroy me."

"That's a bad thing?"

Eli nods quickly, then tugs me down to kiss me. His kiss is different than usual, tender, but deeper in a searching sort of way. We kiss on the blanket until the salt water dries on our skin. Until our lips burn from our feverish kisses. Until finally, I pull away from him, and tug him into the house to shower the ocean off of us. I promised to take him dancing and I'm going to do just that.

Once it's dark outside, I dress in tight jeans and a button-down with my sleeves rolled up. Eli strolls out of the bathroom in skintight black jeans, ripped artfully on his thighs, and a sheer light pink T-shirt. He grins at me as he folds to the floor to pull on a pair of Converse.

"Do I look good?" Eli asks coyly, blinking up at me with feigned innocence.

"Come here." I wiggle my fingers between my spread knees.

Eli doesn't even get up. He crawls towards me, puts his hands on my knees, and blinks up at me with that same doe-eyed expression I'm coming to realize means he's up to no good. I take his curls in a tight grip and yank, forcing his gaze to dip and stay on me.

"Don't look at another man tonight."

"Just you," Eli confirms, unblinking.

"You'll only touch me."

"Only you."

I take his mouth in a bruising kiss, leaving him panting, hard, and wanting for more. I help him up, steadying him on his feet when he sways a little.

"Good?" I ask him, teasing.

"You're going to leave me like this?" Eli asks, frowning, staring forlornly down at his hard cock encased in his tight jeans.

"It'll be worth it tonight."

"It better be," Eli mumbles sourly.

I slap him once on the ass with a smirk, earning me an annoyed look back. Eli heads towards the Jeep, but I stop him with a gentle hand on his shoulder.

"We're not taking the Jeep tonight."

He looks around in confusion for a moment until I pull the cover off the 1967 Ford Mustang. Eli gasps in shock as he looks at the car. Gently, he runs the tip of a finger across the hood.

"What the fuck, Colby?"

"Like it?"

Eli laughs softly. "It's fucking gorgeous. She's yours?"

"Yeah, I restored her with my grandfather as a teen. She's my inheritance."

"Fucking gorgeous," Eli mumbles under his breath. "I get to ride in her?"

"Yeah, baby." I open the passenger door and help Eli in. The awe across his face was worth holding this surprise in. The air is humid when we pull onto the highway, but riding with the windows down is worth it to have the air whipping through Eli's curls. The smile on his face is priceless too. I can't help but reach over to tangle our fingers together.

Eli aims one of those lopsided, blissful smiles at me as we make the drive inland, and my heart is a goner. Four days with him and already I know he's something goddamn special. I want to keep him. How in the world do I even try to lay claim to a wild and beautiful thing like Elijah Ruiz?

The club is dark and full already when we arrive. I usher Eli to the bar with a firm hand on the small of his back. Once we reach the bar, I flag the bartender down, and nod for Eli to order whatever he wants. He orders a shot of top-shelf vodka and I hold my fingers up so that the bartender brings us two.

Eli surveys the crowd while leaning his weight against me. I keep my hand on the small of his back, letting my fingers dip into his waistband just a little. We take the shots at the same time, then Eli kisses me while wearing a blinding grin so that I can taste the liquor on his tongue.

"You gonna dance with me?" Eli asks next to my ear.

The weight of him against me is going to make me do indecent things in public. But I wanted this and I wanted to show him he's mine, even if only for this week. Bodies sway against us in the crowd, but all I can see is Eli. He twists to the beat, curls all over the place, all I can do is try to keep up.

Other people, even couples, stare at Eli. I understand because I can't stop staring either. He's the most beautiful thing on the dance floor. There's an inherent freedom that radiates outward from Eli that others just can't help but notice. That *I* can't help but notice. I'm mesmerized by him.

He sweeps me up with him so that I spend hours dancing with him. At a certain point some other guy tries to dance against Eli's back, but he pulls away when I aim a lethal look his way. Eli notices my look with a laugh, cups my jaw, and kisses me so filthily that I'm afraid we'll catch a charge. I tug him against me so tightly that I think maybe he'll become a part of me.

His laugh echoes against my mouth before he bites my

bottom lip. "I don't want them!" Eli shouts against my ear. "I only want you. My husband."

All the blood in my body threatens to boil. I tangle my hands in his hair and kiss him with everything I have. I dip him on the dance floor, feasting on his mouth, trying to consume every inch of him. He finally pulls away from me, eyes glazed over from the kiss.

"Take me home," Eli says so softly that I almost miss it.

But I don't. I hear him.

I tug Eli out of the bar, ushering him towards the parked car with my arm around his shoulders. He's quiet on the ride home, looking out the window as we ride up the coastal highway. The cloudless sky blinks stars above us and the sound of the waves curls around us.

I lead him inside, a hand on his back, then give him a gentle shove towards the stairs.

"Here's the plan," I say slowly without breaking his gaze, "I want you to go upstairs and get yourself ready. I will give you exactly fifteen minutes to get outside and then I'm going to chase you. I will fuck you where I find you."

Eli doesn't move, he just stares at me from the edge of the stairs. I turn my wrist, look down at my watch, and tap it in clear expectation. That sends Eli scrambling up the stairs. I go to the kitchen, heart pounding in my chest.

I haven't done this sort of thing in years, not since before Marcus. He was never into primal play, he was just barely into my dominant streak at all. Most of the time we made love which fit us just fine. I guess I didn't realize how much I missed this side of myself until Eli unleashed it. I hadn't even intended to be this way with him. Something about him, sweet Eli, just brings it out of me.

After drinking an ice-cold glass of water, I take off my shirt and shoes so that I'm left in only my jeans. The rushing sound of water running upstairs alerts me to the fact that Eli is still getting ready for me. My watch says it's only been a few minutes, so I go over to the piano. I take a calming breath as I sit down.

I let my fingers dance along the keys, playing a song that I don't know the words to at all. The sound of the back door opening and closing is the only sign I need that Eli left the house. Time slows as I look down at my watch, the two final minutes crawling by. Pushing away from the piano, the bench screeches on the wooden floor underneath me. I open the back door to step outside. It's the same cloudless night that it was a few moments ago but the air is full of crackling tension now.

I walk with a purpose to the shore, following the fresh footprints that Eli's feet pressed into the ground as he ran from me. But in a weird way, it feels like he's running towards me. The empty beach stretches in front of me both ways. My heart pounds when I don't see him in either direction. But a noise from the dune to the right has my head jerking in that direction.

"Shit," Eli mumbles, facing me in the dark.

His chest heaves. His fingers nervously clench and unclench at his sides. Even with only the moon to light him up, he's the epitome of perfection. We stare at each other for a moment before Eli takes off at a breakneck run towards the water.

I chase after him, feet pounding the wet sand. Either Eli is tired or he's slow on purpose, but I catch up to him quickly, and topple us to the ground in a heap. Eli lands on the compacted, wet sand with a loud huff. Grabbing his wrists with one of my hands, I hold him still as I unbutton my jeans.

"Please," Eli begs around a moan.

I slip a condom on before roughly slapping my dick against his ass. "You want this?"

"Colby…"

I roughly smack his ass. "Say it."

"I thought you were going to take what you want," Eli bites out from between his teeth.

I push into his tight heat, pushing down on the small of his back so he's forced to take me deeper. God, he's so fucking tight. Waves crash against the shore, mixing with the sounds of Eli's ragged breaths hitting the sand. I watch hungrily as he presses his cheek against the ground, eyes closed, lips parted. Moans of ecstasy slip from his mouth with each of my slow glides in and out of his tight, velvet heat. I thought I'd fuck him hard when I found him but that's not what I want anymore. Not what I need.

I let go of his wrists and roughly tug him up by his shoulders. Sitting on my haunches, I pull him back on my lap so that he's full of me. He lets out a little surprised gasp and presses his hand to his belly.

"I feel you here," Eli mumbles, sounding drugged and out of it. Just from my cock inside of him. "You're so deep that I'm going to choke on you."

I bite off a cry against the ocean water–damp skin of his back. Using my hands on his hips, I force him into a slow grind on top of me, until he's begging me to let him come. God, he feels so fucking good. Made for me almost.

"Please, Colby. Husband. Let me come. I'll do anything." Eli cries out when I take his cock in my hand and give a rough tug. He turns his face towards mine, mouthing at my jaw. "Make me yours. I wish you could come inside me, own me. Nobody else has ever done that. Just you. You can make me yours."

His cries absolutely destroy me. I come inside him with a stifled shout. Eli tosses his head back against my shoulder with his own cry as he comes all over my hand. I hold him in a vise grip, cock twitching inside of him until he slowly relaxes back against me.

"Wish you could stay inside me," Eli says as he glides his fingers over my forearm.

I bite at the damp skin of his neck, softening the bites with openmouthed kisses, then nose at the sweaty hairs. Gently, I pull out of him, hearing him hiss like he did the night before.

"Am I hurting you when we fuck?" I ask, concerned.

Eli tips forward on his hands, tossing an annoyed look at me over his shoulder. "No."

"You'd tell me." It's a demand, not a question.

He shakes his curls so that his face is half hidden from my gaze. "I'd tell you."

His words don't ring true to me though. Would he tell me? I can't be so sure.

I watch as he stands naked under the night sky, a gorgeous figure against the horizon. He lifts his head up to look at the stars, some unknowable emotion spreading across his perfect face. I raise my hand up to touch him, but he backs away out of my reach. Something about that hurts. I feel the loss of him even though he's still standing right there.

"I'll see you in bed," Eli says softly, averting his gaze from mine. "Give me some time to shower?"

I nod in the dark like an idiot. I won't push him, not on

this. He quietly disappears back up the shore towards the house, leaving only his footprints behind. I sit there for a long time wondering how I fucked up. What did I do? My chest feels tight, everything heavy, my body weighted down. Breaths are oddly hard to come by as worry eats at me.

The lights in the bathroom come on in the house, until Eli's shadow appears in the bathroom. I watch with bated breath, as he stands stock-still, unmoving for a long time. Finally, once my lungs work again, his shadow moves as if still in tune with me despite the distance between us.

Never before have I felt such a need to shelter someone inside myself. Keep them safe from harm. Safeguard them from pain or anguish. How am I ever going to let him go?

My heart isn't going to cooperate by the end of this mimicry of a marriage. And I'm not really sure I want it to cooperate. Not anymore.

# 6

## ELI

My body is pleasantly sore upon waking. Stretching out the kinks is wildly difficult with Colby clinging tightly to my back.

Last night was amazing. No one has ever chased me, then fucked me where they found me before. I've done a lot of shit in my time, but that was one thing I've always wanted to do.

Then Colby had to go and turn it romantic.

All I wanted was for him to fuck my brains out by the ocean. Instead, he pulled me to him and ground into me until I saw stars. Until the loss of him hurt.

And he had to care about me too.

No one has ever been so in tune with me before, cared about my pleasure as much as their own. Everything about this arrangement is fucking with my head. I can't be having these sorts of thoughts about my fake husband. It's pretend. I'm *not* a damn rookie.

I carefully wiggle out of his tight hold. When he sleepily reaches out for me, I offer my hand, and let him hold it for a few moments before he falls back into deep sleep.

Quietly padding across the bedroom, I fumble for my phone in the dark. The house is silent when I wander downstairs, just the sound of the ocean wafting through the closed doors.

The sun is just breaking over the horizon. Trevor will be awake at this hour because he's an absurd person who goes to the gym at the crack of dawn. He predictably and thankfully answers on the second ring.

"What's up?" Trevor asks, concerned. The sound of the gym is audible through the phone. His gentle voice soothes my rapid heart.

"Have you ever fallen for a john?"

Trevor inhales sharply. "Eli?"

"Have you?" I whisper angrily.

"Once," Trevor admits wearily.

"What'd you do about it?"

The sound of a door slamming echoes through the phone and the noises of the gym disappear. "I didn't do anything, Eli. I'm a coward. I ran away. I left him behind. Broke my heart and probably his too. If you're falling in love and you think it's real ... Don't do what I did. Hang on to him."

"Trevor ..."

"It's fucking scary," Trevor says, voice trembling. "But Colby sounds like a good guy. I won't tell you what to do though. Just be careful with your heart because I love you. Your heart matters most. How many days do you have left?"

"A couple."

Trevor whistles in sympathy into the phone. "Be careful. I love you."

"Yeah," I agree.

We say our goodbyes, then I go out onto the balcony to watch the rest of the sunrise. It's finally July 4th, but I don't feel the excitement I did just a few days ago. Dread bubbles up inside me because the days are going too fast. I want to hold on to this, even though I know I shouldn't.

Not much later, a gorgeously sleep-rumpled Colby comes down the stairs. It's unfair that he's so sexy when waking up. Makes me wanna fall to my knees right here, right now. I bet he'd let me too.

"Everything alright?" Colby asks, voice sleep husky and lovely.

I hold my hand out to him, gripping his own tightly once he takes mine. I kiss his knuckles, then wrap his fingers around my neck. I aim a smile at him, the best one I've got in my arsenal, and butterflies take flight in my stomach when he grins warmly back at me.

"Everything is great," I lie as my heart starts to form a few cracks.

We spend the morning cuddling on the couch. Colby's fingers gently play with my hair, his new favorite hobby. I lean into it like a cat, soaking the attention up. A rainstorm bubbles up around noon and the house is quickly cloaked in darkness.

"I love rainy days," I admit as a crack of thunder echoes through the house.

"Yeah? What do you do on rainy days?"

"I read."

Colby brushes a kiss against my jaw. "Go grab one of the books I bought and read it to me."

I flush, but do as he says, grabbing my copy of *The Wind in the Willows*. Inexplicably, I want to share this with him. Maybe when he sees this book in twenty years, he'll think fondly of me.

Curling back up against him, I read the book aloud. The

room gets so dark from the storm that it's difficult for me to read the pages. Colby presses a button on a remote by the couch to turn soft lights on around us.

Colby falls asleep a little while later, but I don't stop reading. I read aloud, a little more softly, but I read to him in his sleep in hopes maybe he'll remember my voice when I'm long gone. Maybe he'll remember me after we part, as much as I know I'll remember him.

Another loud crack of thunder startles Colby awake from his short nap. His eyes shift to mine and a sleepy smile is aimed my way, doing my heart dirty.

"Sorry," Colby apologizes, stretching a little. "I didn't mean to fall asleep."

"It's okay." I dip down to kiss his still sleep-soft lips.

"What do you want to do the rest of the day?"

I glance outside at the storm. "Do you think the fireworks are canceled?"

"Definitely."

I can't help but sigh, I was excited to see the fireworks over the ocean. "I've never seen fireworks at the beach."

Colby softly grips my neck with a reassuring smile. "I'll find some on television for you."

"Thank you."

"Anything."

I blink over at him. "Are you happy?"

Colby tilts his head in confusion. "Right now? Yes."

"Before this, before me, were you happy?"

A few beats go by as Colby ponders my question. His cerulean eyes bore into me, trying to figure out why I'm asking such a pointed question. We've carefully sidestepped a lot of things the past few days. Getting to know one another without really getting to know one another. The fake boyfriend curse of knowing one another deeply while staying unknown.

"Most of the time. It's been a tough few years."

"Why?"

Colby takes a deep breath, then lets it out slowly. "My husband died."

"I'm sorry." I mean it too. I am sorry. Even though his husband not dying means I wouldn't have had this snapshot in time with Colby. It seems unfair to everyone all around.

"We knew it was coming," Colby explains with a distant look. His fingers tighten in my shirt for just a moment, enough to tell me the topic is still painful for him. "I had time to say goodbye. I still grieve for him, I miss him all the time, but it hurts much less now."

"You could have anyone. You're smart, successful, beautiful." I dip to kiss Colby's cheeks when he flushes at the praise. God, I love that paint of crimson across his cheeks. "Why'd you have to hire me?"

"I didn't want entanglements ... I need to get back out there, know I could do it, but not have any expectations afterwards."

That confirms pretty much all of my thoughts. Even if I was brave enough to ask for more, I won't. Colby is still grieving and this is practice for him. Practice to get back out there and meet someone worthy of him. Someone smart, someone older, more refined. Someone that can be his equal on his arm. Yeah, I'm going to have my PhD soon, but I'll just be doing research in a dusty basement at a university somewhere once I've got it.

"Let's bake something," I tell Colby with a winning grin.

I skip into the kitchen, rattling through his pantry for anything of use. Luckily, there's an old but still usable box of brownie mix. Colby grabs a large mixing bowl and a baking pan. My sweet, chivalrous helper. He cracks the eggs, I measure the oil and water, then I let Colby stir the mix. We make a pretty good team.

"Want some?" Colby asks, offering me the spatula.

I take a lick, as lewdly as I can, and grin when his hand holding the spatula twitches. Hopping up onto the island, I watch as Colby places the pan into the oven. He sets a timer, then returns to stand between my legs. The warmth of him seeps into me, settling in my bones.

"Hi," Colby says, hands reaching under my shirt to caress my skin.

I shiver helplessly. "Hello," I whisper between us.

"Wanna make out?"

I mock gasp. "Colby Smith! You want to make out with your husband as we bake brownies? Sir, that is delightfully domestic. Yes, kiss me."

Colby laughs, a deep, rumbly thing, before roughly claiming my lips with his own. I wrap my arms around his shoulders, sweetly playing with the golden-blond hair at the nape of his neck. I open my eyes just a little to find his eyes firmly shut, obviously enjoying the kiss. There are some flecks of gray in his hair now that I look closely. I like it. Everything about Colby Smith is bewitching. At least to me.

I get so caught up in the kiss that I forget about the brownies. The timer jolts us apart. We both laugh at the sight of each other, kiss-messy and lips swollen. Colby places a chaste kiss on my lips and I helplessly chase him when he pulls away. He bends over, giving me a delightful view of his ass as he takes the brownies out of the oven.

Colby sets the pan on the stovetop and turns to me with a rakish grin. "Where were we?"

"You're cutting me a piece of that brownie," I say, pointing at the pan, eyes narrowed.

"It's too hot."

"I'll blow on it," I say affronted, giving him my best annoyed face. "Chop, chop."

"You can't be serious. It'll burn you if you eat it right now."

"It cools faster if you cut it," I argue.

With an eye roll of his own, he grabs a plate, and puts a small piece on it for me. I lift the plate to my mouth, making a show of blowing on it a few times. It's blistering hot when I put it in my mouth, but so delicious. I moan around the sweetness in my mouth, gasping when Colby surprises me with a kiss. He licks into my mouth, then pulls away with a triumphant grin.

"That was yummy."

I kick him lightly on the stomach. "I wasn't done."

He blows on the brownie still on my plate with a wicked smirk. Delicately, he lifts a piece to my mouth, and I chew it slowly, just for him to kiss me again. Before long, I'm laughing against his mouth. He repeats this until the small square of brownie is gone. My cheeks hurt from laughing once we're finished.

The storm outside worsens, sending the entire house into gloom. Rolls of thunder and flashes of lightning fill the room. Is my heart breaking in time to the cracks of thunder? Because each day that I spend with Colby will make walking away from him that much more painful.

"Want me to find fireworks on the television for us?"

I shake my head vehemently. "Play me something on the piano?"

Colby laughs lightly. He thoughtfully scratches at his

newly grown beard. "What do you want to hear?"

"Something that you think is beautiful."

Colby sits down at the piano bench, and I sit in the chair off to the side so that I can simultaneously watch him and the tumultuous waves outside. With my legs tucked up under me, I watch enraptured as Colby's fingers glide over the keys. I've never had much of a musician kink, but Colby playing the piano really does it for me. His back is so straight, his fingers nimble across the keys, a gentle, happy look on his face. God, he looks happily lost as he taps the keys.

It takes me a while to recognize the song. "Vienna" by Billy Joel. My mother loves this song. We used to dance around the living room to this song as it played on her record player. Colby sings the words as he plays, wearing some emotion I can't place. I feel absolutely entranced by him. How did he know I love this song? Did he know it would undo me?

He finishes the song and turns to look at me, some sort of raw hope shining in his eyes. I open my arms with what I hope is a tender, comforting smile. Colby comes to me, kneeling between my legs, and hugs me close. Running my fingers through his hair, I hum the song back to him, giving the gift back to him that he so sweetly gave to me.

"That was beautiful, Colby. How long have you played?"

"My grandfather taught me as a boy," Colby admits from where his face is pressed against my chest.

"Were you close with him?"

"Very much. My parents own a business and worked nonstop. My grandfather was retired by the time I came along, so we spent a lot of time together."

"I'm so glad you had him, baby."

Colby bumps his forehead against my chest before lifting his weary gaze to mine. "Can I just hold you tonight?"

I swallow around the sudden massive lump in my throat. His eyes are so sad, so relieved, that I will give him absolutely anything he wants. Anything. I nod and press a firm kiss to his forehead.

"Whatever you want, it's yours," I whisper.

It's late evening, but the storm stops in time for us to watch the sun dip below the horizon. We don't change our plans though. Instead, Colby lies down on the sectional in the living room, and I lay my body over him. His fingers glide up and down my back under my shirt in a gentle caress. The movement is maddening because of how much it thrills me.

"What's your favorite food?"

I turn my head on his chest to look out at the waves. "Pizza."

"What kind of pizza? Are we talking cheap delivery or wood stove?"

"There was this Italian place down the street from my grandparents' house that made the old-fashioned real pizza. The bread was thin but soft. And they used the thick slices of mozzarella cheese on top, not the shredded stuff. God, it was so good. Just thinking about it brings up some of my best memories."

"It sounds amazing," Colby agrees, fingers playing with my curls. He loves to do that. My curls are his catnip.

"What about you?"

"I love a good bowl of ice cream."

"That's dessert!"

Colby smacks my ass with a chuckle. "It's a food, brat."

I shift a little to look him in the eyes, trying to look as annoyed as I can. "Pick something that's not a dessert."

He huffs, eyes glinting with mischief. "I love pickles."

"Pickles," I repeat in shock. "Pickles?"

"Yeah, the ones in the barrels at the grocery stores."

I gag at the thought. "You can keep your pickles."

He just shrugs. "More for me."

I lie back down on his chest to stare out at the horizon. One of his hands rests at the small of my back, a comforting weight, while the other cards through my curls. I must nod off because it's dark when I wake up. A flash of color bleeds into the room, followed by a boom, and I gasp when I realize it's fireworks.

"Colby!" I excitedly shout as I roughly shake him awake.

He blinks up at me in sleepy confusion, then angles his head to take in the fireworks. "Well, I'll be damned."

We shuffle out onto the balcony to watch the fireworks. I lean against the railing with a smile tugging at my lips. Fireworks! God, it makes me feel like a little kid. Colby wraps an arm around my shoulders, pulling me tightly to him, and I tilt my head against his chest. What a perfect day.

Colby pulls his phone out of his pocket and puts on a playlist of slow songs. Nothing I immediately recognize. He pulls away from the railing, spinning me so that he's holding me in the cage of his strong arms. With one arm around his shoulder, and my other hand held in his, he guides us in a slow dance as the fireworks pop in the sky.

"What's a dream you've always had?" he asks as he looks tenderly down at me.

"To dance in front of the fireworks at the beach," I murmur helplessly. The truth is that my dream has always been to be romanced, to be loved, and Colby has been slowly making that dream come true these past few days. The fireworks are the easiest truth I can offer him.

A teasing smirk tilts his lips up. "Really?"

I nod up at him, biting my lip. "Yeah, husband. You?"

His hand tightens on the small of my back, bringing me closer against the warmth of his body. "I've always wanted kids. I grew up in a big, loving, southern family. Marcus never wanted them though. He was my dream, so I gave my other dream up for him. But I've thought about it a lot since losing him. Having kids. I think I'd be a great dad."

The way he sounds so sad, so wistful for a future he's not sure he can have, absolutely tears me apart. I wish I could give him that. I hope he can have that dream one day. I need him to have it.

I kiss his cheek, then nuzzle my face against his. "You've still got time. Maybe one day."

"Yeah," Colby says sadly. "Maybe one day."

We dance quietly for a little while longer, until the fireworks finish. But we hold each other long after we've stopped dancing. I try to wrangle my wild heart, but it's a stallion that won't listen to my fervent pleas to behave.

# 7

## COLBY

Complete and utter perfection. Those words don't do last night justice. Not even close. Last night was *beyond* perfect.

The joy on Eli's face just from the fireworks ... I wish I could put that look on his face every day for the rest of my life. His smile lights up his entire face, like the fireworks lit up the sky the night before. Then we slow danced. My sometimes still fragile heart beat like a stampede of wild horses in my chest as I held him and swayed to the pop of fireworks.

Eli is still sound asleep beside me as the sun works its way higher into the sky. I glide my fingers down his flank, smiling when he sighs happily in his sleep. He presses closer to me and I take a deep breath of his hair. The intoxicating scent of salt water and sunshine still somehow lingers on him.

The absolutely wild thought that I want to keep him floats through my head again. I want to keep Elijah. I want to live every day like this, with him in my arms. But we've purposefully kept things vague as we've gotten to know one another.

I know only the most basic and mundane facts about him, about his mother, about the accident that caused the gnarly scar across his perfect knee. I don't know if he does this on a full-time basis, what he wants to do with his life. I don't even know if he'd be interested in something more with me.

Also, I'm not an idiot. I'm sure every man that does this with him falls in love, because how can they not? He's the epitome of husband material. Eli makes me laugh, makes me feel free in a way I haven't in years. The man also makes me decidedly possessive. If he does that for everyone he "dates," then undoubtedly many men have fallen in love with Eli.

I still don't know how I can keep a wild and perfect thing like him. But I want to try.

I press a kiss against his hair with a weary sigh. Pulling him closer by a hand on the small of his back, sleep claims me again with him tucked safely against my chest.

---

THE NEXT TIME I AWAKE, the sun is shining brightly through the room. I'm confused for a moment, about what woke me up, but then the wet suction around my cock sends a zap of sizzling lightning down my spine. Movement under the blanket along with a quiet moan, has me burying my fingers in Eli's curls.

"Such a good boy," I murmur into the soft quiet of the bedroom.

Eli licks at the head of my cock, then dives back down to swallow me whole. I arch off the bed, forcing my cock deep into his throat. A gasp escapes me when Eli chokes before letting out a deep moan that feels delicious around my cock.

Oh, he likes that. Of course he does. Using my fingers buried in his hair, I force him down onto me for a few seconds, then drag him back up.

His fingers tighten against my thighs as I keep fucking his throat until I'm just about to come. I try to warn him, to pull him off, but he just takes my cock deeper in his throat as I let out a long, satisfied moan. My orgasm rockets through me, sending my cum right down his throat. Eli sucks me until I'm shivering with sensitivity, then he pulls off, reverently kissing the tip of my cock. Like I just gave him the most precious gift.

I tug him up to my mouth by my tight grip on his hair. He gasps against my lips as I lick the taste of myself out of his mouth. Eli tastes like us. So perfect, so honest.

I pull away from his mouth and laugh when he chases after me.

"Come up here," I demand as I tug him until he's kneeling over my face. God, the sight of him trembling over me, hair wild, eyes blown with lust makes my cock wish it could go again.

"Now fuck my mouth."

"Colby," Eli gasps, eyes round and wide as he looks down at me.

I slap his ass, making Eli whimper. "Be a good boy and fuck my mouth. I won't tell you again."

Eli nods, his breathing harsh as I take his hard, leaking cock into my mouth. He tastes divine. He tastes like Eli and the ocean and everything good in this world. His thighs tremble beside my head as he thrusts deeply into my mouth.

Years of practice have made it easy to take him into my throat, swallowing around him on each thrust. I stare up at him in awe as he buries himself in my throat over and over again. Eyes rolling back into his head from pleasure, thighs trembling, hands tightly gripping the headboard, he paints a vivid picture of pleasure. He's the most beautiful thing I've ever seen.

My fingers dig into the meat of his thighs, probably hard enough to leave bruises. I don't think Eli will mind though. A gasp leaves his mouth as I swallow around him. Some emotion that I can't parse crosses his face as he looks down at me. His head hangs down as he hungrily watches his cock disappear into my mouth. He licks his lips and rolls his hips, making me gag a little.

One of his hands falls from the headboard to sweetly cup my jaw. His thumb presses against my lips, feeling the slide of his cock in my mouth. The expression on his face knocks all the air from my lungs. He looks swept away just from the sight of me. I have never needed someone to come down my throat so badly before, not as badly as I need Eli.

"Yeah, suck me," he whispers, voice shaky.

I suck him down harder, then use my tight grip on his hips to force him to quicken his thrusts. His cock hardens in my mouth and he whimpers. Eli looks so wrecked, so debauched, that I wish I could take a picture of this moment to keep forever.

He comes like that with a quiet gasp, shivering, thighs trembling beneath my fingers. I swallow him down, wishing for more once it's over. Eli falls to the side, panting harshly, then reaches over to lightly pat my face.

"Best cocksucker on the planet," Eli says, voice awed.

A loud, barking laugh escapes me. I roll over and place a sound kiss on his mouth. "Come on, husband. Let's take a shower and start the day."

Eli shakes his head, still panting from his orgasm, but still eagerly follows me into the bathroom. We take a slow, decadent shower, washing each other gently without any heat since it's been burned out of us. He smiles softly at me as he carefully washes his messy curls and my heart does that traitorous skip again.

I wrap a fluffy towel around Eli once we're out of the shower, then proceed to tenderly wipe the cascading drops of water from his golden skin. He rolls his eyes at me but lets me do it all the same. I'm learning that's just Eli's way with me. It's been a long time since caretaking someone brought me this amount of peace, of joy, and I appreciate Eli in a way I'm not sure I can ever properly explain to him.

I place a sweet, closemouthed kiss on the scar of his knee, and look up at him through my lashes. Eli blinks down at me, fingers twitching rapidly at his side.

"Husband," I whisper against his soft skin.

Tears well up in Eli's eyes, and his bottom lip trembles. I stand in a rush and cup his cheeks in the palms of my hands. He tries to wrestle from my grip but I hold tight, unwilling to let him go until we've talked.

"What's wrong?"

Eli shakes his head wildly in my grasp. "Nothing. I have allergies."

"Eli," I say, reprimanding him for the obvious lie.

"Colby, don't." Eli sniffs once, then places a sweet, chaste kiss against my palm. "Make me feel special today. Give me the husband experience. Can you do that for me?"

That I can easily do. I kiss him softly until the tension leaves his body and he sways against me. He leans against me, like he was made for me, like my body was made to protect him.

We get dressed in comfortable clothes due to the oppressive heat we'll undoubtedly encounter outside. Florida is predictable in the summer.

Eli looks like a showstopper just in frayed denim shorts, a T-shirt for a band I have no idea about, and beat-up Converse. He looks so young, in a way that makes me feel wildly protective of him. His age reminds me that the gulf between us is so similar to the one between Marcus and me. But age doesn't matter when souls recognize one another, right? It had worked out so well for me before. Even though the age gap had been reversed.

Eli climbs into the Jeep with a smile that shakes me to my core. God, I'm going to miss that fucking smile. We drive down the coast to only the sound of the wind in our hair. After we pull through a drive-thru for coffee, Eli puts his hand on my knee, almost out of habit. I swallow against the rising tide of emotions inside of me.

I take him to a local sprawling garden so that we can walk around with our coffees. Eli tangles his fingers with mine and swings our hands back and forth between us.

"It's not too hot out this morning," Eli comments while taking a slow sip of his iced coffee.

"Probably the rain from yesterday."

Eli hums thoughtfully. "Probably true."

"Where did you grow up?" I ask because I need to know more about him.

Eli turns to me, eyebrows knitted. "Why? You're my husband, you know already."

"Eli."

He laughs, that deep, beautiful laugh that I want to bottle up. "We moved around a lot actually. I've lived mostly everywhere. But I live in the South now."

"Where?" I demand, tugging on his hand so that he has to face me. "Tell me where you live now, Eli."

"Don't do this," Eli whispers. His eyes implore me to stop. "Colby, be good to me today."

I swallow against the feeling of him slipping away from me. Eli falls into my arms easily when I tug him to me, wrapping an arm around his waist, one around his shoulders, I hold him close to me. I kiss his wild curls and breathe him in deep.

"Sorry," I say into his hair.

"Forgiven," Eli mumbles into my chest.

His fingers curl against my side just once. He pushes me away and grins brightly up at me. "Where is the butterfly garden?"

I tenderly push some curls from his face, letting my fingers linger at the edge of his forehead, then trail them down to press my thumb against the dip of his lips.

"I'll show you," I tell him.

Eli quirks his head, smiles, but doesn't reply. I take his hand back in my own and tug him towards the butterfly garden. The butterflies are so active today, flying all over the place. Must be the humidity. It's an open garden, full of bright, blooming flowers. Sweat breaks out across Eli's back, dampening his shirt. I watch as he strolls through the garden with a large grin on his face. That awed look crosses his face as he sweeps his fingertips across the blooming flowers, lingering on some bright blue hydrangeas.

A butterfly lands on his outstretched hand. He gasps in happiness, then turns to look at me, nodding towards his hand so I see the butterfly.

"I see, baby," I say, voice strained even to my own ears.

Eli doesn't notice that I'm about to break down. I pull out

my phone to snap photos of the moment, wanting to capture it forever. The picture can't capture the purity of the moment though. Not by a long shot. The butterfly lifts off and flies away. Eli watches it until it disappears from his sight. I can't help but feel like Eli is that butterfly for me. Giving me a few moments of awed bliss, before flying away to better skies.

This hurts more than I ever thought it could.

We spend the rest of the early morning walking through the gardens. After we're done there, we hop back into the Jeep, and head towards the local pier. It's a tourist trap, but it's fun too. I want to show Eli the best that there is to offer here. I try not to think about why.

The pier is pretty packed considering it's the day after the Fourth, but it's worth it. We shop and I spend money on Eli even though he tries to stop me. I buy him souvenir items to remember his time with me. We buy matching hats because they have manatees on them which oddly makes Eli smile.

The last store we wander into is a jewelry store, with expensive beach-themed jewelry. I'm sure we look a sight, but the sales people must be used to people like us wandering through the store. Eli stops at a glass case of ocean-themed necklaces in varying shades of gold. He smiles down at them, before moving on. I grab his forearm to stop him.

"Pick one," I tell him softly, out of hearing of the nearest sales person.

Eli swallows, throat bobbing. "That's too much."

I shake my head fervently. "I want you to take something with you. I need to do that for you. Let me?"

Eli purses his lips, but nods without argument. For which I am very grateful. He spends a while perusing the glass case, before settling on a gold conch shell on a matching chain. It's beautiful.

I wave at the sales person that's been watching us a few feet away. "We'll take the gold conch shell."

The salesperson nods and leads me over to the register to check me out. It's not crazy expensive, but it's real gold, so I know it'll last as long as Eli is careful with it. Which I know he will be. Once we're outside of the store, I take the box out of the bag, and pull the beautiful necklace out of the cushioning.

Without a word, I spin Eli around, and tenderly place the necklace around his neck. His fingers come up to play with it, his lips tipping up in that smile that I know means I did good. Pushing those pesky curls out of his gaze, I dip down to kiss him chastely, just a sweet press of mouths.

Finally, after we've bought bags' worth of things we definitely don't need, I take him out to the edge of the pier.

"No one's fishing?" Eli asks with a frown.

"No, because people swim here. They don't want to attract sharks."

Eli nods in understanding. "Makes sense. What are we going to do with the rest of the day?"

I lean against the railing, looking out at the horizon. "I kind of want to just take you home and have you as many times as I can."

"Sounds good to me," Eli replies. He bumps his arm against mine so I look over at him. Eli looks at me tenderly, eyes shining sweetly, like he knows everything I'm not saying.

So, I take him back home. The house that I had purchased for me and Marcus suddenly feels less like a reminder of what I lost with him, and more of a reminder of what I'm going to lose with Eli. I'd purchased the beach house as a surprise for Marcus but he never got to visit. The cancer came out of nowhere and stole him from me so quickly. Diagnosis to hospice in the matter of months.

I'd wanted to bring him here but never got the chance. An odd part of me is grateful that I never did. Although it was purchased for us, for him, now I'll always remember this week with Eli when I visit the beach house. This one perfect week.

# 8

## ELI

The final day with Colby is the sweetest torture I've ever known. He took me to a garden so that I could stand among butterflies. I'd watched them fly around me, into the sky, one even landed on me. But what made it even more perfect was the way Colby had watched me. The look in his eyes when his gaze landed on me was something else. I felt every inch of his gaze like a caress.

Then he took me to the pier, bought me anything I so much as looked at. Bought me that damn necklace that I'll never take off. He'd walked me to the edge of the pier and told me he wanted to take me home to have me. He had sounded so in need that I hadn't been able to deny him.

I don't think I'll ever be able to deny Colby. I don't want to either.

We return to the house just in time for dinner. I leave Colby in the kitchen to cook. It doesn't take long for me to get ready for him. After so many years, it's a routine that I have down easily. Music echoes around the kitchen when I come back downstairs. The sound of my feet padding along the wood floors has Colby turning to look at me from where he stands at the stove.

He aims a breathtaking smile my way and in that instant I know I'm forever fucked.

It took five days for me to fall in love with this man. How many days will it take for me to fall out of love? My stomach churns at the idea of doing this with anyone else. Just the idea of being touched by someone else makes my heart clench painfully in my chest.

"Can we eat dinner later?" I ask quietly, suddenly feeling shy.

Colby's gaze is hot on me, but he nods tightly, then covers the pans on the stove, turning the burners off. He stalks towards me, all heat, want, and need. Taking my face in his large palms, he kisses me possessively. All the air leaves me in a rush when he licks into my mouth, owning me with his lips. My cock aches just from one simple kiss with Colby.

His hands trail down my back and cup my ass, lifting so that I'm forced to wrap my legs around him. I gasp into his mouth as he carries me up the stairs to the bedroom. Warm sunlight casts the bedroom orange. Colby gently lays me on the bed, following me down with his body, kissing me with an urgency that I've never experienced before.

His mouth devours me and I just try to hang on. I curl my fingers against his back, digging my nails into his skin, hoping to leave marks there long after I'm gone. Colby tears himself away from my mouth to trail kisses down my neck and chest. Moans flow freely from my mouth because my body has a mind of its own.

Colby's lips leave a wake of fire behind them as he kisses down my stomach. His fingers hook into the band of my underwear, tugging them down without any fanfare. My cock slaps against my stomach and I tangle my fingers into the sheets to stop myself from dragging Colby back to my mouth.

But he knows.

Colby stands and hurriedly undresses himself as I watch on with lust-hazy eyes. He's so fucking beautiful. The soft, blond hairs that cover his firm muscles. His blue eyes that devour me at every chance they get. The heart inside his body that beats away for someone else, the heart that I wish was mine. Colby Smith is everything I've ever dreamed of having, but never dared to wish to keep.

I lick my lips when I look down at his hard cock.

"You want my cock?" Colby asks as he climbs back onto the bed. He flips me over easily, manhandling me onto my knees. He bites one of my ass cheeks, sending a thrill coursing through me. But the kiss he places on the bite soothes the momentary pain. "You want me to fuck you hard? Fuck you sweet? What do you want, husband?"

I swallow down a cry. "Sweet," I admit softly, embarrassment flooding me.

"Of course, you do, baby. My good boy. You want me to show you what it means to be my husband?"

I nod against the bed and force my eyes to stay dry. I won't cry. *I will not cry*, a mantra that I repeat in my head until my body believes it.

Colby licks my ass tentatively a few times, as if he's savoring the taste of me. Then he just dives in. He eats me with a fervor that almost scares me. Every lick and swipe of his tongue sends me keening, begging for something that I don't think he can even give me.

*Please, more, now, so good*, are the only words that fall from my lips as he eats me alive. When he pushes a lubed finger into me, I almost scream in frustration. I just want him inside me. I want him so deep that no one else will ever be there again. I want to feel him in my throat.

"Please, Colby, please. Husband," I cry as he continues to finger me and eat my hole. My thighs tremble as I fight back my orgasm. I could come just from this, just from his mouth and fingers. He's going to be my ruin. No one else will ever fuck me like this, have me trembling for them, quaking with need.

Colby grunts loudly and kisses up the curve of my spine. I expect him to press into me, fuck me on my knees, but he doesn't. He flips me over and kisses me so that I can taste where he was on his tongue. God. I reach down to grasp his cock, giving it a good squeeze. He's already wearing a condom and he's wet with lube. Oh, God. He's going to fuck me like this, on my back, legs wrapped around his waist.

He breaks away from my mouth with a pained groan. Steadying himself with a forearm by my head, he grasps his cock and guides it to my hole. He watches with lust-blown eyes as he sinks into me. God, he's so big. The stretch is beyond anything I've ever felt before. I feel so full of him even before he bottoms out. Maybe we were made to be like this together.

Tilting my head back against the pillows, I firmly shut my eyes against all the emotions flooding through me. Once he's buried to the hilt, he kisses my trembling lips. I dig my fingers into his biceps just for something to hold on to, so I'm not swept out by the tide.

His pace is slow and gentle, making me cry out in frustration. I try to spur him on faster with my heels, but he just chuckles darkly. He grinds into me, not even thrusting, just torturing me. Colby grips my jaw with his fingers and forces me to meet his heated gaze.

"You wanted slow," Colby reminds me.

I grit my teeth in irritation. "Slow, not glacial."

He grinds into me again, making me see stars. Every slow glide in and out deliciously tugs at my rim. Colby abruptly freezes deep inside me and I swear I can feel him in my throat. I watch in confusion as Colby lifts to his knees, but my confusion melts away when he grabs my hips tightly and tugs me up, forcing me to straddle his waist as he sits on his haunches. Our faces are only inches apart in this position. Our panting breaths mingle together in the darkness of the room.

"Ride me," Colby demands before laying a possessive kiss to my slack mouth. "Take what you want."

My body knows what to do before my brain does. I grind against him as I curl my arms around his shoulders, burying my fingers in the sweat-dampened hairs at the nape of his neck.

I keep the pace slow, just a gentle grind, but my orgasm still sneaks up on me. Lightning zips down my spine, fire spreads throughout my body, and I know my orgasm is close, but I don't want it to end. I don't want this lovemaking to be over. Because that's what this is if I'm honest with myself. Colby is making love to me even though I'm the one taking his cock at my own pace.

He stares up at me, so fiercely full of desire, that tears spring to my eyes again.

"Tell me," I whisper against his mouth as he fucks up into me.

"Tell you what?" Colby mumbles distractedly, like he's too caught up in me to even think.

"Tell me I'm a good husband. Tell me I'm the very best."

His breath leaves him in a giant woosh. "Eli," Colby gasps my name.

"Tell me," I beg as a lone tear escapes down my cheek. The tear visibly breaks something inside Colby. I watch as his face goes through numerous emotions in the space of seconds.

Colby keeps one hand on the mattress to steady us, but uses the other to tenderly cup my jaw. I tilt my face into the palm of his hand as I keep a slow grind on his cock.

His fingers dig into my jaw as he unflinchingly meets my gaze. I think he sees me, really sees Elijah Ruiz. Not the sex worker, the PhD pursuer, or son of a single mother, just ... Eli. When I'm with Colby I'm nothing else but his.

"You're the best husband," Colby vows, voice trembling with restrained emotion. "I'm so glad you're mine. My husband, my Eli."

I gasp as my orgasm rolls through me like a wild wave crashing against the shore. My vision whites out for a moment, but I don't miss the way Colby comes right after me, bucking so far into me that I think maybe I will feel an echo of him inside me forever. We gasp for breath together for a few moments, just staring wide-eyed at one another. Shocked by the intensity of the moment we just shared.

Colby jostles us a little so he can take my face in both of his hands. The look on his face is just south of adoring. "My husband, my Eli."

Tears fall from my eyes because I can't hold them back any longer. Colby sweetly wipes the tears away with his thumbs, and kisses me lovingly while still buried deep inside me. Only when he softens enough to slip out do we break apart. No words are exchanged between us as Colby gently guides me into the bathroom. I don't think any words would even do if we tried.

He draws a bath and fills it with bubbles that smell like tea tree oil. The bathroom fills up with steam as I look forlornly out the bathroom windows. The sun has disappeared, gone below the horizon. Gorgeous pinks and purples fill the sky. A beautiful end to a beautiful vacation. Because that's all this was, all this ever could be. A vacation from real life for both of us.

Once the bath is full, Colby sits down in the tub, then helps me into the bath between his legs. I lean my back against his solid chest. His fingers card through my curls, pulling the knots out that formed during our lovemaking. Relaxation flows through me enough that I feel myself drift a little, not to sleep, but into a state of relaxation I've never quite allowed myself before.

"My husband," I whisper sleepily, just as sleep overtakes me.

---

I WAKE up once during the night. My mind is a scattered mess until I remember where I am. My brain immediately goes a mile a minute.

What am I going to do about this man who brings me breakfast in bed, buys me books, learns my every tell, and is starting to feel more like a real husband than a fake one? How am I going to return to my life back in Georgia and know that Colby is off living a life that I'm no longer privy to? And how am I going to fall asleep at night without the weight of him against my back keeping me grounded to the earth?

None of these questions can be answered by my pea-sized

brain. I wonder if Colby has considered the same things or will life go right back to normal for him once we go our separate ways?

The very idea almost knocks the wind out of me. Just the idea that he will watch me walk away tomorrow without a care in the world could stop my heart in my chest. I can't think about it now though. As my mother always says—those are tomorrow's worries, so there's no use borrowing trouble for today.

I turn into his arms and bury my face in his neck. He lets out a pleased sound in his sleep before laying a heavy arm over my back. I let myself fall asleep in his arms, comforted by the weight of him, without worrying about how tomorrow night I'll be sleeping alone in a bed that won't smell like him.

Darkness greets me when I blink fully awake for the final time. Colby is a solid weight against my chest. Sweat covers our bodies from us being pressed tightly together.

Today is the day we have to go our separate ways. The final day.

The worst part of me wants to flee while Colby is asleep. Take the coward's way out. But that's not fair to either of us and that's not what Colby paid to have this week. The husband experience can't end with one of the husbands fleeing during the night.

So, I just lie there and listen to Colby breathe. His breath puffs against my neck on each exhale, tickling the skin of my neck. I grip his arm around me while I watch the sky change slowly as the sun rises on the other coast. The sky goes from black, to dark blue, to pink, and finally light blue as the day comes for us.

I know Colby won't sleep much longer because he's an early riser. Moments later, he jolts against my back, proving me right. Despite everything, I smile to myself. Gentle hands roll me over so that Colby can look down at me. A bittersweet smile graces his own lips.

"I thought you'd leave before I woke up," Colby admits sheepishly. God, how can a man that fucks like the devil be so sweet, even shy at times?

"I wouldn't do that to you."

Colby sighs and tightly shuts his eyes. "I don't think I can watch you walk away."

"Then you won't watch me walk away," I whisper against his stubbled check. I lean back just enough to brush a close-mouthed kiss against his lips. "Make me breakfast, hubby?"

We take care of morning business together in the bathroom. Brushing our teeth together at the sink and grinning at one another in the mirror. Downstairs, Colby makes me waffles again, and fruit without any berries. I devour the waffles because Colby is an amazing cook. An amazing man.

We're quiet as we clean up the kitchen. I wonder if Colby is going to stay here or leave when I leave? What will he do once I'm gone? What life will he go back to? Colby stays downstairs as I return upstairs to pack my things. I'm leaving with more than I brought, not just in belongings. I'm leaving here a man in love. A professional fake boyfriend that fell for the client. Pathetic, I know, but it's now my sorry lot in life.

To know a love so pure if only for a few days, is something I will treasure for the rest of my life.

Colby's out on the balcony when I come downstairs with all my belongings. Just like that first day. How was that only six days ago? It feels like a lifetime. Colby turns and takes in the sight of my suitcase, of me standing unsure at the edge of the living room. Some emotion that I can't name crosses his face.

*Ask me to stay*, I think. *Ask to keep me*, I ache to beg him. But I don't. Just like people have tried to own me before, I don't want to put that back on him. I don't want him to be forced to ask for something that he might not even want.

Instead, I open my arms, and hold him tightly against me. We sway together in the living room. His arms are a tight band around me as I breathe the clean scent of him in. Expensive cologne and the ocean. Is it silly for me to ask him the brand name? I want to ask him so that I can buy it and spray it on my pillows, but I know it won't be the same. The scent won't have the hint of Colby that should accompany it.

Colby presses a tender kiss to the edge of my jaw, then pulls away. Quietly, we walk out of the house towards my car parked in the driveway. My heart beats like a hummingbird's wings in my chest. Is this how it feels to break your heart in real time?

I unlock my car and Colby loads my bags into the trunk for me. When he comes back, he stands in front of me with his hands in his pockets as if to stop himself from reaching out for me.

"My husband, my Colby," I tell him around the emotion threatening to choke me.

Colby closes his eyes on a pained sigh. "My husband, my Eli."

"Hey," I whisper, forcing him to look at me. "Don't watch me go. Pretend I'm going out for groceries and I'll be right back, okay? I'll be right back."

"Okay."

"What ice cream do you want?" I ask around a bitten-down cry.

Colby blinks rapidly in confusion. "What?"

"Ice cream," I repeat mechanically.

Understanding dawns on Colby's face and tears swim in his eyes. Damn. If Colby cries there is no way I'll be able to leave him. I'm not a praying man, but I send a quick prayer for those tears to stay in his eyes. Please.

"Cookies and cream," Colby answers with a trembling voice.

"Two pints of cookies and cream. I'll be right back."

Colby swallows so hard that his throat bobs painfully. I watch with tears in my eyes as he turns and heads back towards the house. He freezes on the steps with a hand on the railing, back a tight line under his shirt. With my breath caught in my chest, I climb into my car, and slowly back out of the small driveway. Colby never turns around, not that I can see at least. And I watch for a long time in my rearview mirror until Colby is only a speck.

Nothing has ever hurt this bad before. Why does leaving Colby feel like I'm leaving my heart behind? An almost physical pull to turn around, to throw myself into his arms, wrestles inside me. So, I do the only thing I can think of to do.

I call my mom.

"Mama," I cry into the phone as I navigate towards the interstate.

"Angel! What's wrong?" she asks gently, and suddenly I miss her so much. I haven't seen her in person since Christmas. Sometimes, all a boy needs is a hug from his mom.

"I just left Colby. But I didn't want to leave him. I think ..." I take a deep breath, then blow a raspberry as I come to a stoplight. "Can you fall in love in just a week?"

Mom hums thoughtfully into the phone. "I fell in love with your dad in only days, it's not my fault he didn't deserve my love. Sometimes people don't. But this Colby sounds special if he could make my sweet Eli fall in love with him. Turn back around!"

"It was a job, Mama."

She scoffs, making me laugh despite my tears. "You're not as good an actor as you think, angel. Everyone that meets you falls in love with you. They have your entire life. You're just not so good at realizing it."

Her words have the desired effect on me, the tears stop. Silence fills the car for a little while as I drive. Comfort radiates through me just by having her on the phone with me.

Maybe I could give it a few months, then reach out to Colby? I can be brave. There's always the possibility that this week meant as much to him. Actually, that's a lie. I know this week meant something to him because Colby isn't an actor at all. He's the one who wanted the week to be real, didn't want me to act at all.

A few more red lights separate me from the interstate. Once I've got cruise control on and I'm heading towards Georgia, maybe things will feel better. The more space I put between us will make it feel less like I'm leaving my heart behind, beating outside of my body.

"You want to stay on the phone the rest of your drive? Or you want to be alone a little bit?"

I sigh and wipe at my tearstained face. "Tell me about your week."

I push through the final red light, heading towards the interstate, when I notice a speeding vehicle cutting through traffic. Wait. Is that the Jeep? My heart practically flies out of my chest. I slow down, and my heart stops when the Jeep pulls up alongside me. Colby's shouting something but I can't hear him through the window.

Rolling the window down, I'm met with a look of relief washing over his face. "Pull into the gas station!"

"Who was that?" Mom asks as I do as Colby said, parking by the air machines.

"Colby," I say in wonder. "Mama, I gotta go. I'll call you back later."

Mom just laughs as I press the end button on the steering wheel. Colby parks the Jeep right behind me, then appears at my door, chest heaving and a sight for sore eyes. Despite having just seen him not even ten minutes ago.

The moment I unlock the door, he roughly tugs it open. His gaze is so heavy, so distraught, concern momentarily overwhelms me. I quickly jump out of the car and cup his cheeks in my palms, rubbing my thumbs under his eyes.

"Hey, what happened?"

"I can't do it."

Butterflies take flight inside me again. But I temper myself. Stay calm. Life is not a movie.

"Can't do what, Colby?"

He tips his cheek into my palm. "I didn't watch you walk away but I felt the loss of you. I felt it in my heart, in my bones. I know this is crazy, it was just a week, but goddamn it, Eli ... I think you're supposed to be mine."

Wow. I stare at him in the middle of the gas station parking lot. He stares back at me expectantly, but without an edge of hurry. My always patient Colby.

"You know this is completely crazy, right?" I finally ask.

He nods in total agreement, letting out a high-pitched laugh. I pull my hands away just in time for him to run his own hands roughly over his face, then through his hair. The sandy-blond locks stand up on top of his head. I realize for the first time today just how tired he really looks.

"Yeah, I'm very aware of how crazy this is but that doesn't mean it's not real."

He's got me there. I nod softly and look down at my feet for a moment, gathering my courage. Someone honks behind us, but I barely hear it. All I can hear is the pounding of my heart and Colby's soft breaths as he anticipates my words.

"It was real to me too," I admit softly, unable to look at him.

"Thank fuck," Colby bites out, before tugging me into his arms for a world-shattering kiss. It's not a filthy kiss, there's no tongue, nothing dirty about it, but it's probably the best kiss I've ever had. Because this kiss says, *you're mine, let me keep you, this is real*. I try to say it back with my mouth, with the bite of my fingers against his biceps.

Finally, Colby pulls away, fluttering kisses across my cheeks, making me laugh.

"Stay with me?" Colby murmurs against my temple. His fingers toy with the curls at the back of my neck as I lean all my weight against him.

"I have a life in Georgia, one that will take time to uproot." But I will uproot. I'll alter my entire life just for a chance at something real with Colby.

"Georgia." Colby laughs a little hysterically. "We've been so close this entire time. I live about four hours East of here."

My nose wrinkles. "In Florida?"

Colby laughs at me, the laugh that makes me smile because it's so damn infectious. So real. So honest.

"That's your blueberry face. The idea of living in Florida makes you have the blueberry face."

"I will make a sacrifice for you."

He kisses me again. Softly, just a chaste press of mouths. "I'd uproot my life to Georgia, but my family is here. There's been a lot of change the past year for them, I don't think they could take that too."

I shake my head and rise up on my toes to hug his shoulders. "Florida can work. I'll have to see about transferring to a college here since I'm mid-program, but it can be done."

Colby freezes, all his muscles going taut under my hands. "The agency said you were twenty-eight."

I chuckle and pull away to look up at him. "I am. I'm getting my doctorate."

His face practically glows. "A doctor?"

"Yeah," I confirm, suddenly embarrassed, feeling a flush spread across my cheeks. "In English literature. I want to do research or teach ... I haven't made up my mind yet. But for now I do research and teach a few classes. The school subsidizes paying for the PhD program and pays me to teach."

His hand rubs down my spine, then lands possessively on the small of my back. I suddenly realize we're having this entire conversation at a gas station. Looking around, I'm grateful that no one is paying us an iota of attention. Could go either way in the South really.

"Can you spare a few more weeks with me? Stay with me in Florida. Meet my family. See my house. Then we can decide what to do from there."

More time with Colby sounds amazing. I'm not sure I can say no to him. And I realize with startling clarity that I don't *want* to say no to him. So, I don't.

"Okay, husband. You can take me home."

## 9

### ELI

After one more perfect day at the beach, we pack up our cars, and I follow Colby back to his home. The landscape outside my window changes from coastal, to oak trees heavy with moss, hills, and billboards that make me vaguely uncomfortable. But I roll the windows down and try to keep the nerves inside me at bay.

I still think this is all kind of wild. We fell in love in a week, but maybe love is a wild thing worth chasing. Maybe it is possible to fall in love so quickly, especially when that someone is Colby Smith. The hard thing, the real test, will be if we can make it work as just Colby and Eli. Not as pretend husbands.

Finally, we turn onto a paved road in the middle of nowhere. A gate opens and I follow Colby's classic Mustang through it. Oak trees line the driveway, for what feels like forever, until a large, white farmhouse comes into view. The sight of it takes my breath away. Trees surround the house, and there's even a front porch with rockers on it.

Late afternoon sunlight shines behind the house and I am

in love. In love with the man who brought me here, the man who built this house, and with the idea of the future we could have if I give it a chance.

Colby hops out of the car with a smile, making my heart do somersaults in my chest. His stupid smiles are going to make me develop a heart condition.

He opens my car door for me, helping me out with a hand on my forearm.

"This is my home," Colby says with pride.

"Did you design it?"

Colby nods as he looks at the house. Pride radiates off of him too. "I designed it after Marcus died. I couldn't live in the home we shared together anymore. It hurt too much. So, I sold that house, and finally built my dream home." He uses his arm to gesture around the property. "This is my family's land, and I was given these ten acres when I turned eighteen. I always knew I'd do something with it, I just didn't know when."

The front door opens and a dog comes racing out at us.

"Who's this?" I ask, dipping down to give them pats.

"Whiskey, she's my best girl."

"Whiskey," I murmur, laughing when she licks my face. Her hair is long, and almost auburn. "What kind of dog is she?"

"Irish setter. She was a gift from Marcus, towards the end."

Colby's voice isn't sad, just informative. We have so much to talk about and Marcus is one of them. I wish we had talked about him more at the beach house, but I never had the courage. Never really felt right. But if I'm going to start a life with Colby, then I need to know about the man who safely kept his heart before me.

*The Husband Experience*

A man comes out of the farmhouse, hands tucked into his pockets. He's a giant of a man, even taller than Colby, but he's got dark hair where Colby's is light. The man waves at us from the front porch.

"That's my cousin Beau. He's been dog-sitting for me."

Colby takes my hand and pulls me towards the front of the house. Whiskey runs around the yard a few times, doing her business like a real lady. She comes back to bounce excitedly at Colby's feet. I totally get it. He laughs at her, giving her loving pats on the head.

"She missed ya," Beau says as he watches Whiskey jump around. He's got a southern accent just like Colby, but his voice is a little deeper, and his southern accent is just a little thicker.

"She was good?" Colby asks, squeezing my hand.

Beau nods. "Course. I kept her at my house, but brought her back here today when you said you were heading home." Beau sends an unsure look at me, then aims his gaze back at Colby. "All good?"

Colby lets go of my hand and hugs Beau, who stays stiff the entire time, but sweetly pats Colby on the back. When they pull apart, Colby looks back at me with a teasing smile on his lips.

"This is Elijah. He was my fake husband, but I think maybe one day he'll be the real thing. If he'll consider it."

I can feel the flush spread over my cheeks, and warmth diffuses through my entire body. Half embarrassment, half in pleasure. This man is going to be the absolute death of me.

Beau whistles, tipping back on his heels. Must be a family thing.

"Nice to meet you, Elijah." Beau puts his hand out, and I shake it firmly. His hand eclipses mine. I'm not even a small guy, these guys are just superhuman big. But they're kind and sweet too.

"You can call me Eli," I tell him with a gentle smile.

"Alright, Eli." Beau nods, then looks out at the sun behind the trees. "I better get back to my place. It might be the middle of the week, but we're ramping up for the weekend at the farm. You gonna bring him by?"

Colby lets out some sort of noise that Beau takes for agreement. Beau trots down the stairs with a dip of his head in my direction. He just walks down the paved driveway, then hops over the gate, and goes across the street. Weird.

"Where is he going ..." I trail off and look over at Colby.

"He lives across the street."

"I didn't see any houses."

"Well, across the street means something a little different here," Colby explains. "It's about a thirty-minute walk home, but it's good for him. He likes solitude. If he needs to get somewhere in a rush, then he takes his truck, but that's usually only to go to work. Otherwise, Beau walks."

How interesting. Whiskey lets out a bark and nudges at Colby's hand. With a wide smile, eyes crinkled at the corners, Colby pushes open the front door. "Wanna see inside?"

Duh. The inside of the house is just as beautiful. Dark wood floors gleam from the sunlight shining in through the broad back windows. Everything about the house inspires comfort, putting me at immediate ease. A wide porch spans the back of the house, with more rocking chairs, along with tables for company.

The backyard expands out as far as I can see with trees dotting the land. A few hills away there's another farmhouse, but otherwise it's just us out here. Something about that sends a shiver down my spine. Colby lets me wander, so I do.

*The Husband Experience*

I go from room to room, inspecting the house that Colby designed and built for himself, for his future. The idea that he wants to bring me into his dream home makes me feel special. Makes me feel a part of something bigger than myself.

The long hallway leading to what I assume is Colby's bedroom is lined with photos of his family. A photo of a young Colby with Beau and who I assume is another cousin captures my attention. God, Colby has always been beautiful. Easily twenty years old, Colby looks younger, but the smile is exactly the same. His smile has always been infectious and full of life.

The picture next to it has a smiling Colby in a suit, with an older man in a matching suit. He's got pitch-black hair, dark eyes, and a smile that looks like it doesn't come out a lot. But it's no less happy, no less ecstatic.

"Is this Marcus?" I ask quietly.

Colby comes up beside me, a steady presence. "That's Marcus."

"You look so happy."

"He made me very happy." Colby turns me so I'm facing him, hands firm on my hips. His fingers dip under my shirt, sweetly tracing the warm skin he finds there. "He made me so happy and I'm so grateful for the life that I lived with him. But that doesn't negate my ability to love you too, to build a life with you here. If you'll have me."

Emotions clog my throat. I let my forehead fall to his chest. Colby lets me gather my thoughts, doesn't push me to speak before I'm ready. His fingers continue their gentle onslaught against my skin, calming me more than he'll ever know.

"Alright, Colby. The husband experience was fun, but we

need to start at the basics. We need to date and get to know one another, and try to make this something that can last. Okay?"

Colby chuckles and runs his palms higher up my back, under my shirt, before cupping my shoulders. His warmth bleeds into me and I lean against him more, letting him take my weight.

"We can be boyfriends for a little while before we do the husband thing for real."

I roll my head back and forth on his chest while I laugh. "You're infuriating. Alright, so we're downgrading one another to boyfriends."

"A demotion," Colby says seriously.

I nod seriously. "Demoted."

Colby tugs me away from his body to kiss me thoroughly. I sway on my feet a little, but he keeps me close, kissing me so possessively that my brain short-circuits just a little bit. I blink up at him in a daze when he pulls away.

"My boyfriend, my Eli," Colby murmurs against my slack mouth.

"My boyfriend, my Colby."

We kiss again and it feels like its own sort of vow. A promise that I hope to keep reaffirming for many years to come.

# ELI'S EPILOGUE
## AUGUST

This is it. The real true test of my relationship with Colby. The combination of our family and friends. Mom is beside herself with joy at the idea of finally having more people in our small family of just two. Although I'm not sure Whiskey is included in her ideal-family combination.

Whiskey obviously doesn't get the hint. She adores my mom, follows her all over the yard. I watch in amusement as Whiskey follows my mom while she checks out the trees, the garden, even the perimeter of the house.

"It seems safe," Mom points out as she shoos Whiskey away with her elegant fingers.

"It's very safe here, Mama. I promise."

She wiggles her nose at me in distaste, her eyebrows scrunched. "It's just very far out in the middle of nowhere. Won't it be a long drive to school?"

"About forty minutes. I think it's worth it."

"Well, if you're happy," Mom relents. Her long blonde hair, with a few hints of gray thrown in, cascades over her shoulder. My mother is the definition of elegance and sweetness. I know she's going to fit in perfectly here.

Colby comes out onto the porch with a shy grin. He raises his arm and waves at us like a total dope. And my heart dips and dives all over again just because of that.

Mom laughs. "You're such a sucker for him."

"I am," I admit without glancing away from Colby.

"Howdy," Colby calls out from the porch. "What are y'all up to?"

"I'm checking the perimeter for ways that perpetrators can gain access."

Colby looks stumped. "Okay."

"She watches a lot of *Dateline* and listens to a lot of murder podcasts."

Mom sniffs delicately. "One can never be too prepared."

Colby actually looks a little worried. "I have an alarm system. Whiskey barks when the wind blows. Did you notice anything? I can have the alarm company out here tomorrow."

I laugh and run up the steps to him. He tosses a distracted arm around my shoulder and stares my mom down, waiting for her answer. Mom relaxes a little at his words. Absently, and without knowing, she even pats Whiskey on the head. Which makes Whiskey's entire bottom half shake like she might take off from the ground.

"It is fine, Colby. I think Eli is safe here with you."

Colby smiles and glances down at me. "Good," Colby says before pressing a kiss to my nose.

"Breakfast for dinner?"

Mom nods her approval. She walks right up the stairs, past us, and into the house with Whiskey on her heels.

"That dog is in love with her," I say fondly.

"Hmmm, yeah."

Colby tips back a little on his feet. He checks to make sure Mom is out of view, and pushes me against the railing of the porch. The next minute his lips are on mine, devouring me, tasting me like he didn't just kiss me this morning. Mom came in last night and she's been staying with me in the mother-in-law suite above the garage. So, we've been missing each other an extra amount lately. Especially after a few weeks of bliss between the time at the beach house and the farm.

His thumbs tilt my jaw so he can deepen the kiss at the angle he wants. I let him without putting up an ounce of fight. Sagging against the railing, he pushes his body against mine, all heat and possession.

"I love you," I mumble against his mouth.

"Mmmm, I love you too. Gonna sneak into my room tonight?"

"No sneaking!" Mom yells from inside the house.

Colby basically jumps out of his skin and immediately puts enough room for Jesus between us. The southern gentleman in him runs deep. Even the idea of doing anything slightly naughty with my mom present could send him into a conniption. Something about that makes me love him even more though.

"Mom!" I whine, feeling like a teenager all over again.

"Not while I'm here!"

Colby huffs out a breath. "She'll be gone after the party tomorrow, right?"

I nod and blink slowly at him. "Uh-huh."

He nods a few times, rubbing his hand over his jaw. "Good."

I laugh at him, then kiss him softly, before turning to

head inside. I pause with one hand on the doorframe to look back over my shoulder at him. "I feel like giving chase a little bit."

Colby's pained groans follow me into the house.

---

THE NEXT DAY is just south of chaos. Twenty of Colby's closest family members, my mother, and my best friends fill Colby's backyard. Whiskey is moderately calmer and better behaved with Colby's cousin's service dog in attendance. Although her tail still beats a rapid tattoo against the ground as she sits waiting for the other dog's attention. Poor girl.

I carry a plate of food out onto the porch, carefully placing it with the other food on the table. Out of the corner of my eye I spot Colby and Beau chatting quietly as they ready the grill for the food. A smile tugs at my lips at the sight of them too. After my few weeks here, I've learned just how close they are. Basically brothers and it shows in how they live across the street from one another.

Beau stops by all the time. Colby will stop by Beau's place on his way home to me from his firm downtown. It's very nice. Beau has warmed to me the past few weeks and I've come to appreciate the man.

"You think the best quarterback of all time is ... Jimmy Garoppolo?" Jackson asks incredulously. His voice is just a little overloud, which I know means he's rattled.

Benji's laugh echoes across the yard, so I follow it to stand with my friends under the glorious shade of an oak tree. A few of Colby's younger cousins are happily standing around chatting with my friends.

"He's hot," Harper, Colby's cousin, says with a mild shrug.

"You can't rank quarterbacks solely on their hotness," Jackson accuses.

Harper's eyes narrow. "Says who?"

Jackson looks so puzzled that I can't help but laugh as well. Benji makes a bomb-exploding motion with his hands and I have to hold in a joyful squeal. I'd missed my friends so much. Moving to Florida was the best option for me to try this thing with Colby out, see if we can make something permanent from it, but I miss them more than I ever could've imagined. If only I can get them all to move to Florida with me.

I wish Trevor could've made it. He never answered me, but I'd hoped he'd come. I haven't seen him for months either. His absence in my life has been so loud.

Jackson's horrified groan brings me sharply back to the present.

"You rank all football players on hotness?"

Harper's grin is absolutely devilish. "I rank all athletes on hotness."

"I think you've 404 errored Jackson," Benji notes around a mouthful of chips.

"Sounds like an accomplishment," Harper says with another shrug.

I survey the crowd again, before letting my gaze fall on Colby. Our eyes meet because he is already watching me. For a moment he looks sheepish, but my smile and wave have his face transforming into something else, something warmer, something just for me.

Movement at the edge of my vision has my gaze moving behind him, towards the edge of the house. I'd know that long blond hair and gentle smile anywhere. Just as I'm about to make my way over to Trevor to greet him, Beau shoves the grill tongs into Colby's chest, and jumps the porch railing to seemingly attack Trevor.

What the hell? Just as I'm about to make a run to stop it, Jackson's hand on my arm stills me. He shakes his head and nods for me to look back in their direction. Beau tramples Trevor to the ground, a hand tenderly cupping the back of his head, and they're whispering something that none of us can hear. Not sure I'd even want to hear really. The moment feels so special, so private, that I feel like an invader. Even more so when Beau intimately kisses Trevor for all of us to see.

Wait.

"Is that ..." I trail off.

"The one that got away," Jackson says softly, an edge of tenderness in his voice.

"Oh wow."

Beau pulls away from Trevor with a grin that can rival the most Hollywood-grade smiles. They don't even bother coming to the party, instead disappearing beyond the house. I'm dreadfully nosy, so the disappointment is real that I'll have to wait for the full story.

"I guess Beau's boyfriend came back?" Harper wonders as he looks at the now empty patch of grass.

"Boyfriend?" I repeat blankly.

Harper nods as he turns his gaze back to us. "They dated last year? He was here for Andy's wedding and then for the funeral. Haven't seen him since though. I think he was still in college."

So many things are now adding up. Beau's the john Trevor fell in love with? This is a mystery that I will be solving. In time. When Trevor is ready to give me all the details.

The party goes on despite the reunion we all witnessed. Food and friendship and family. There's not much more anyone can ask for at the end of the day. By the time everyone is gone, even my mother, the whole property is dark. Only the sound of the cicadas echoes around us, a sound that I never knew I could love so much.

Colby grabs my face in his palms and tugs my mouth to his own. I moan against his mouth, then sag against him in utter relief. He easily holds my weight like always.

This man is my entire future. I know it in the marrow of my bones, in every beat my heart skips just by being in the same orbit as him.

"Still wanna be chased?" Colby mumbles against my mouth.

"Kinda want something else," I admit.

He pulls away to push my hair from my forehead. "Tell me what you want and I'll give it to you. Anything. Don't you know that by now?"

I smile up at him, fingers gripping his shirt tightly. "I know."

Colby only lifts one eyebrow in question.

"Make love to me?"

Colby doesn't reply with words. His response is to sweep me off my feet and carry me to his bedroom as I laugh at his antics. Before Colby, I didn't know what making love was. I didn't know that someone can take their own pleasure in my pleasure. But I do now.

"My Eli," Colby murmurs as he curls around my sweaty body.

"My Colby," I whisper back to him.

## COLBY'S EPILOGUE
### ONE YEAR LATER

My first wedding was a grand affair. Marcus had a lot of friends and family, so the wedding was over one hundred people in a ballroom in the city. I loved that day, it's still one of my favorite days. But today is going to be special to me in its own perfect sort of way. A favorite day for a different reason.

I stare at myself in the full-length mirror for a few heavy beats. Officially forty and starting all over. More wrinkles line my face this go-around, more life experience under my belt—a lot more loss too—but Eli was worth all of that to have this second chance at love. Eli's the wild thing that I never want to tame. Getting to keep him still feels unreal.

After our week at the beach, Eli spent a few more weeks with me at the farmhouse. We were intentional about dating, finding out if we fit outside of the bubble of the beach house. Thank fuck, we did. Also, thankfully he was able to transfer for the fall semester to be closer to me so we could do it all for real. Not everything was easy though because life rarely is.

He moved into the mother-in-law suite above my garage. He paid me rent too. That was a hard-fought battle, which Eli easily won. But by Christmas he'd moved into the house with me and we'd settled into a routine. Into a life. I'd taken him to the beach house for a few days over Christmas break and asked him to marry me. His watery grin had been perfect, so perfectly Eli, that my heart mended just a little bit more that day.

And today he's officially becoming my husband.

"All set?" Beau asks from behind me.

I tug at my tie one more time before turning around. Beau's decked out in a suit, which is a rare occasion for him. Only weddings and funerals can wrangle him out of his Levi's and ball cap.

"I've been set for a while," I say around a wide grin.

Beau claps my shoulder to steer me out of the bedroom. "Don't cry before the wedding."

When I'd asked Eli the type of wedding he'd wanted, he'd sighed dreamily and said *intimate, something just for you and me and our closest family.* I know I've accomplished that when I look out over the crowd. The backyard has a handful of people scattered around. My parents, Beau's mom, our other cousins, aunts, and uncles, Eli's mom, and a few of his friends. All in all, there's maybe forty people seated in my backyard, which is just perfect for us.

Beau walks towards the end of the aisle to stand in the middle, the model officiant. I'm so glad for our friendship later in life, Beau's not just my cousin, but my best friend. I don't wait long for Eli under the old oak tree. The sun shines through the foliage, shadows moving as the summer breeze blows about the branches heavy with moss. Eli's smile is blinding as he walks down the aisle to join me, dipping to give his mother a kiss on the cheek.

"Hey, boyfriend," Eli whispers to me, a cheeky smile on his lips.

"Hey, I'm being promoted in a matter of moments."

He shyly bites his lip and takes my hands in his own. "You're right. Let's get a move on, then."

Beau laughs, so does everyone else in the small crowd.

"Today, we're all here to witness Eli and Colby becoming husbands. They've elected to forgo the traditional process, instead wanting to speak from the heart. So I'll keep this brief and let them speak. Once they're done, I'll make it official."

I squeeze Eli's hands as I stare deep into his beautiful eyes.

"When I was a kid, there were fires all over the state. I remember helping the family soak the earth at the farm and our roofs at home in case the fire got too close. It was terrifying, packing a suitcase to prepare to run from the flames. But we got lucky and our land stayed untouched." I pause for a moment to smile at Eli as he visibly wonders where the hell I'm going. "Afterwards, my grandpa took me out to the burned forests to show me the destruction. It was awful. The trees had scorch marks for years. But what I remember most is finding flowers or weeds growing through the scorched earth. That's what you are to me. New life after destruction, when it's finally time."

I bite back tears because we both swore we wouldn't cry. But Eli's eyes swim with tears, and I know that he won't be able to hold them back. I have to tell him though, at least just once.

"I'm so lucky to have known two great loves in my life. I

wake up every day so excited to hear your laugh, to tease you, even to be sad with you because I know I'm safe with you. You are a million rainbows after every storm. I promise to never put blueberries on your breakfast tray. I promise to hold your hand on dates." I squeeze his hand with a watery smile. "I promise to sweep you off your feet as long as I'm alive because you deserve every ounce of romance I can give you. I promise to give you my all, to give you my best, and to love you until the day I die."

Eli rubs his tear-sodden cheek against his suit jacket and squeezes my hands tight. He blinks up at me a few times, centering himself. I can't help but lean down to kiss him, softly, then press my forehead to his before pulling back away to let him say his vows.

Eli takes a deep breath, releasing it out slowly. "I'm supposed to follow that up?"

The crowd laughs and it's just so ... Eli. The love I have for him is boundless. He winks at me.

"I fell in love with you at first sight. My brain just had to catch up with my heart. You are everything I ever wished for in a partner. I can't wait to spend the rest of our lives together, going on adventures, slow dancing, doing puzzles, reading to you so that you can fall asleep." I chuckle, and so do a few people out in the crowd. Eli squeezes my hands tightly a few times before plowing on. "Making you laugh and smile is one of my greatest joys. I promise to do my best to make you laugh every day, even on the hard days. I promise to never run away from you, but towards you, because you are my reason to run. My reason to keep going. My everything."

A tear falls down my cheek, but Eli pulls a hand away from mine to wipe it away with a tender smile that calms my racing heart.

"On that note," Beau says with a lot of emotion. "Eli, do you take this man to be your lawfully wedded husband?"

"I do," Eli says brightly.

"Colby, do you take this man to be your lawfully wedded husband?"

"I do," I repeat gruffly.

Beau claps his hands once, grinning at the both of us. "By the power vested in me by the great state of Florida, I now pronounce you husband and husband. Kiss!"

Beau doesn't have to tell me twice. I take Eli's face in my hands and press a smiling kiss to his own grinning mouth. My husband. Eli laughs against my lips before tangling his fingers in my hair to kiss me just a little harder, tasting my mouth like he didn't just kiss me this morning. I'm out of breath when I finally pull away. Eli blinks up at me, dazed like he always is after a kiss, so I press another tender kiss to his temple.

Our friends and family clapping in the crowd pull us out of our temporary overjoyed bubble. We spend the next hour or so taking photographs between the oak trees in the backyard. One of my cousins is a wedding photographer, so she's doing it for us as her wedding present. I can't wait to hang one up beside the photo from my first wedding to showcase the two loves of my life.

Once the photos are done, we're both a little sweaty because of the heat. We join our friends and family on the back porch. Beau's got the grill going, my dad has a beer in his hand, and my mom is happily chatting it up with Eli's mom. It's lovely and perfect.

"Hey! We both got promoted. I think that calls for celebration." Eli wiggles his eyebrows suggestively. "Chase me tonight?"

He's teasing, I know he is, but I don't feel like teasing. I pull him against me, smiling at his gasp, and take his mouth in a warm, bone-melting kiss. As he always does, he relaxes against me, letting me hold up his weight. My hand lies hot and possessive at the small of his back, tugging him as close as I dare in front of our friends and family.

The beaming smile he aims my way is practically blinding when I finally pull away from him. I use my other hand to brush an errant curl from his forehead.

"I'll chase you forever," I tell him honestly.

Because it's true. I'd chase him to the very edges of the universe just to keep him.

"My husband, my Eli." I teasingly tug on a curl, letting it go so it pops back into shape.

His eyes practically sparkle. "My husband, my Colby."

And then I kiss him again because I can, because he's *mine*. I'll burn for him forever, until the end of our days. Loss might be a part of me, but I've learned a valuable lesson the past few years. Sometimes beauty sprouts from the most painful of losses. Like the first flower to bloom from the scorched earth after a blaze. All proof rests with Eli. My forever wild and beautiful thing.

### The End

Pre-order Trevor and Beau's book now! Releasing in September.

Join my Facebook Reader's Group to be the first to hear about upcoming new releases, WIP's, and teasers. Subscribe to my mail list to know about new releases.

If you enjoyed this book then please leave a review whenever you review books. That's how indie author's like me get found. Much appreciated.

# ACKNOWLEDGMENTS

To my husband, who held me for countless nights as I wept over Just a Footnote. You've seen me through many storms and we've come out the other side every time. To more sunshine and laughter and unbridled joy.

A special thank you to all that read this before it was edited and when it was just a stream of consciousness: Amber, Lexi, Devin, and Donatella. You girls are irreplaceable.

To my friends that have become siblings and soulmates. I don't need to name you. If you read this and think "is that me?" Then yes it's you. You're my rainbows after the storm, the promise of ever afters.

To Hannah Henry for your unwavering support and cheerleading even through the destruction. I'm honored to call you a friend.

To those that asked for more. Well, here you go.

And finally my forever thanks to Aiden. You will always be a permanent part of me. Burned into my soul. You were loved by a few for a short time and I am so glad you received the love you deserve but have trouble accepting. I'll love you forever, the character that carries my soul inside him. We survived.

# ABOUT THE AUTHOR

Maya spends most of her time imagining happily ever afters for the characters that live in her head. If she's not plotting how to heal broken hearts for her characters then she's spending time with her devoted husband and precocious daughter. She loves baking competitions, listening to the same song on repeat for months, and discussing the latest pop culture event in a group chat with her best friends.